THREE ALARM FURY

FEDERAL BUREAU OF MAGIC COZY MYSTERY,
BOOK 6

ANNABEL CHASE

RED PALM PRESS LLC

CHAPTER ONE

I EXAMINED myself in the full-length mirror set against the wall of the attic. Black wings. Eternal flames in my eyes. Yoga pants. Okay, the yoga pants weren't a new fury trait, but they seemed to show every sin from my butt to my ankles.

"Come on," I said, twitching impatiently. "Where are you?"

"Right here." Alice Wentworth popped up behind me and I jumped forward, nearly falling into the mirror.

"A little warning next time," I said, and resumed my position.

"I'm so sorry, Eden. I thought you were asking where I was."

I cast a glance at the ghost over my shoulder. "No. I'm hunting for my new fury trait. There has to be one after this last incident."

"Incident?" Alice repeated. "You mean when you killed yourself on the Day of Darkness to save the town from a spore demon and your family resurrected you? That incident?"

"Yes, that incident." I returned my attention to my reflection. "I guess there are some traits that aren't physical. I can't see my strength by looking in the mirror. Maybe it'll be another enhanced ability." Fingers and toes crossed.

Alice hovered beside me, gazing at my reflection. "Can a fury trait be a perkier bosom?"

I cupped my boobs. "You think they look perkier?"

The ghost scrutinized my chest. "Mmm. Maybe not."

My arms dropped to my sides. "Fury traits are never attractive qualities. It's not like I'll get a rounder bottom or smaller feet."

"Immortality is pretty attractive," Alice countered. "Some people would kill for that."

"But I get eternal flames for that one and not the kind The Bangles sing about," I said. "Couldn't my eyes just be a brighter color instead? Less flecks around the iris?"

"Eden..." Alice drifted away from me. If she was any whiter—well, she couldn't be any whiter. She was already a ghost.

"What's wrong?"

Alice pointed at my head and released a high-pitched squeal.

I glanced back at my reflection and there it was—or, more accurately, there they were.

Snakes.

I screamed.

Three of them were entwined in my hair. They twisted around long, dark strands, their forked tongues flicking in and out. One of them deposited a stream of venom right into my cleavage. Gross.

"Are they detachable?" Alice asked.

Now wasn't the time to think practically. "Someone get these melon farming snakes off my melon farming head!" I yelled.

They hissed in response to my tirade.

"Go away!" I commanded. I was suddenly thirteen again and ordering my brother out of my room. When I looked back at my reflection, the snakes were gone. My body sagged with relief. "You saw them, right? I didn't imagine them?" Though I wished I had.

"On the bright side," Alice said, "Charlemagne will enjoy his new playmates." Charlemagne was my niece's Burmese python that lived full-time in my mother's house. The enormous snake was more puppy than reptile though. He liked nothing better than to curl up beside you on the sofa with a toy that he could sink his fangs into. He was also a big fan of Cheez-Its. I discovered that the hard way when I left a bowl of them on the end table in the family room.

I stared at my head, now back to its normal inky black with a hint of frizz. "This is a disaster."

Alice floated over to console me. "Never mind. A brush will fix that."

"I'm not talking about *this* hair." I groaned in exasperation. "I sacrifice myself for the town and this is my reward? Medusa hair?" Life was so unfair.

"Can yours turn people to stone?" Alice asked. "If not, I think you should request an upgrade."

I glared at her. "The Federal Bureau of Magic would not look kindly upon their agent turning humans into stones."

"No one will see them unless you choose to uncloak them," Alice said. "Might be a nice ace in your pocket when someone steals your parking spot at Christmas."

"Alice! I'm not using my fury powers to frighten humans for petty reasons."

"You're right. It's a terrible suggestion, but I would find it entertaining. Being a ghost can be so boring sometimes." She coasted across the floor to gaze out the window. One of her favorite spots.

"I'm sorry," I said. It couldn't be easy for her. The last

Wentworth had owned this property decades ago and Alice had been left behind—in her apparitional form, of course. Now that I was immortal, I'd be 'left behind' someday too.

Alice looked at me. "There I go making this about me when it should be about you. I think I'll make myself scarce. Go downtown to the library and see who's reading in the ghost section."

"Please don't scare anyone."

"A few books on the floor," Alice said. "What harm can it do?"

I exhaled, resigned to let her have her fun.

By the time I dragged myself downstairs to the kitchen, my family was assembled around the table, enjoying fresh oatmeal with sliced bananas and cinnamon.

"What's the matter with you?" my mother asked, the moment she laid eyes on me. The witch seemed to possess psychic abilities when it came to her only daughter. Then again, my entire family seemed to be immune to my poker face.

I took a seat next to Aunt Thora. "Got a little gift from the gods today. Ugliest bow you've ever seen."

The witches stared at me expectantly as Princess Buttercup, my hellhound, came loping into the kitchen.

"Hang on. She needs to go out." I scraped back my chair.

"Not until you tell us about your gift," my mother said.

I stood. "I'll tell you when I come back, unless you want her to pee on your favorite rug."

My mother's eyes flicked to the hellhound. "Her pee is acidic. Last time she had an accident it burned a hole straight through to the hardwood floor."

"I rest my case."

"You don't need to go out with her," Grandma said. "That's what the fence is for. Open the door and let her out, then come back and tell us before I hex it out of you."

Why had I opened my big mouth? I could've kept it a secret. Well, I could've tried. It wasn't easy to keep a secret from my nosy family and I already had a more important one to keep.

"No need for hexes, Grandma." I escorted Princess Buttercup to the back door. "No digging or jumping over the fence. Just come straight back and bark."

The hellhound darted outside and I returned to the table.

My mother straightened, her eyes sparkling with the kind of enthusiasm she usually reserved for delivery men. "This is so exciting. I feel like I've won a prize."

"That's how you felt when you and Stanley realized you'd given birth to a fury, remember?" Grandma asked. She tipped back her head, enjoying the memory.

"We thought we'd won the supernatural lottery," my mother confirmed. "Anton was wonderful, of course, but we knew he was a vengeance demon like Stanley. Then came our infernal bundle of joy." She smiled at me in a rare moment of maternal adoration. "And then she grew old enough to speak and demonstrate free will." Her adoring smile faded from her coral-stained lips.

"And she was forever a disappointment, yada yada," I said. "I know the rest of the story." I lived it every day in fact.

"Go on, show us," my mother urged.

"Yeah, hurry up. It's Little Critters community day," Grandma said. "I need to go downtown for a few challenges." Grandma had become obsessed with the game on her phone and was routinely upsetting every kid with a Little Critters account in Chipping Cheddar.

I rolled my neck and uncloaked my new trait. I heard the hiss of the snakes and shuddered. Charlemagne heard them, too, because he came slithering into the room in search of his new friends.

Grandma whistled. "That's quite a unique look you're adopting."

"You're hideous," my mother breathed.

"Gee, thanks." I cloaked the snakes and Charlemagne dropped his head back to the floor in disappointment.

"Furies were frightful creatures back in the day," Aunt Thora said. "They weren't beautiful but deadly like sirens and mermaids. They were simply ugly, birdlike goddesses that tortured men."

"In other words, my soul sisters," Grandma said.

"At least Eden is able to wear her human skin most of the time," Aunt Thora added.

I cut a glance at my great-aunt. "When you say it like that, I sound like a serial killer."

"Be grateful, dear. Your ancestors didn't have the ability to cloak their appearance," Aunt Thora said. "They had to endure it day in and day out."

"They also spent their days pursuing the wicked around the world and exacting punishments," I said. "A lot has changed."

My mother gave me a pointed look. "Has it though?"

"If I were pursuing the wicked to punish them, this house would be empty," I said.

"Can I see them again?" Grandma asked. "Let me take a photo with my phone for posterity. I want to use portrait mode and brighten the green of their scales."

"So you can post it on social media?" I asked. "No thanks."

"What?" Grandma asked. "Just last week, Ginny Featherstone posted a photo of her grandson. The kid had a forked tongue. Do you know how many likes it got?" She pointed to my head. "Snake hair will trump that kid's forked tongue by at least a hundred likes."

"You're not memorializing my snake hair to 'win' on social media," I insisted.

"And here I thought you were competitive," Grandma grumbled.

"Not when it comes to *that*." I started for the back door.

"Aren't you going to eat the oatmeal?" Aunt Thora asked.

"I've lost my appetite," I said. "I'm going to find Princess Buttercup. She probably wandered over to Dad and Sally's hoping for a treat." Despite my protestations, my father spoiled the hellhound with food she shouldn't eat.

"Oh, sure," my mother muttered. "Go show off to your father and his emotional vampire."

"Actual vampire," I called over my shoulder. I shut the door behind me and whistled for Princess Buttercup. When she didn't come running, I walked the five hundred yards across the property to my father's house. My parents divorced when I was ten and, as part of the settlement, they split the land in half. My mother kept the original farmhouse that had once belonged to Alice's family and my father built a new house on his lot. I'd spent a good portion of my childhood running back and forth between the houses and acting as an emissary between two adults who despised each other. It was no wonder I escaped Chipping Cheddar the moment I got the chance.

I banged once on the kitchen door of my father's house before waltzing in. My father stood at the kitchen counter, about to give Princess Buttercup his Belgian waffle.

I folded my arms. "Are you seriously feeding my hellhound human food at the kitchen counter?"

"What? She loves it. Watch." He tossed the waffle into the air and she snatched it into her powerful jaws like a shark latching onto a seal.

"I know she loves it," I said. "That doesn't mean she's allowed to have it. No more."

"You're so restrictive," my father complained. He turned to look at me. "Why are you wearing that shirt?"

I glanced down at my T-shirt that read—*when life hands you lemons, make a gin and tonic*. There was an image of fresh lemons next to a tall glass.

"What? Aunt Thora bought it for me. It's cute."

He turned his attention back to the other waffle on his plate. "Makes you look like an alcoholic. You don't want to turn into your mother."

I groaned. "Mom is a lot of things, but an alcoholic isn't one of them." Narcissistic. Evil. Oversexed. There was a definite list.

"Well, don't wear it to work," he said. "It's unprofessional."

"My office is comprised of Neville and me and it's situated between a donut shop and a tattoo parlor," I said. "The shirt is fine."

Sally swept into the kitchen, slipping a pearl earring through her lobe. "I thought I heard you, Eden. What brings you here at this hour?"

"She was here to snatch a single moment of joy from Princess Buttercup," my father said.

I rolled my eyes. "You're ridiculous."

"Speaking of ridiculous," my father began, "Sally said she saw you filling up your car at the place on Mozzarella Street the other day. How much did you pay?"

"I don't know," I said, as casually as I could. I already knew that was the wrong answer.

My father narrowed his eyes at me. "You don't know? You're so wealthy on that public servant salary that you can afford to play Russian roulette with gas prices?"

"It's hardly roulette. There's a certain range of reasonableness and I'm well within it."

"How do you know if you don't check?"

"Because no one is evacuating from a hurricane and Jimmy Carter isn't president," I said.

"Why didn't you go to that place on Asiago? It's two cents cheaper."

"Because that's in the opposite direction," I said.

"But it's two cents cheaper."

"And I'll spend that two cents driving out of my way to get the cheaper gas."

"Stanley, give it a rest," Sally said. "Not everyone obsesses about the price of gas." She looked at me. "You know your father. He doesn't want to be taken advantage of."

I laughed at the thought of someone taking advantage of my family members. That was basically taking your life in your hands.

"I need to show you something," I said. Now that I'd shown the other half of my family, I knew I had to reveal the latest trait to my dad and Sally or there'd be hell to pay. The rivalry was too great to ignore.

"An engagement ring?" Sally asked hopefully.

"Who would she be engaged to?" my father boomed. His voice was always ten decibels louder than it needed to be. "She's not even dating anyone."

"That's right," I said quickly. "Not dating at all. Much too busy." I couldn't possibly tell them that I was dating Chief Sawyer Fox. They'd never approve of a human and the chief would never approve of my ethically and morally bankrupt family.

"Well, you're immortal now," Sally said. "Plenty of time for dating."

"I doubt anyone would be interested in dating me like this." I uncloaked my head and the snakes wriggled on my head. One slid down to rest on my shoulder, peering back at their audience. With their open mouths and round eyes, my father and Sally were clearly stunned.

"That's the most beautiful thing I've ever seen," my father said in a reverential tone.

"Mom called me hideous."

"I'm sure she meant it lovingly," Sally said, knowing perfectly well that Beatrice Fury meant nothing lovingly ever.

"This is because you killed yourself?" my father asked.

"Use power, get ugly," I said with a shrug. "That's the fury way."

Sally reached toward me. "Would you mind if I touched them? Their fangs are exquisite." She showed her own set to the snakes and they quickly settled.

"They're pumped full of venom," I said. "One of them burned my boobs earlier."

Sally stroked one of their heads. "Such divine creatures. You're very lucky, Eden."

"Yes, lucky," I said in a small voice. I could only imagine Chief Fox waking up next to me when I'd accidentally uncloaked my traits. He'd leave a man-shaped hole in the door on the way out.

"Stop hunching over," my father scolded me. "Stand up straight. By the devil, you have a crown of snakes. Wear them with pride."

With pride? Inwardly, I sighed. Only my family.

"Come on, Buttercup," I said. "Let's go home." I needed to head into town sooner rather than later.

The hellhound looked from me to the counter. She seemed reluctant to leave the waffles behind.

"No waffles," I said. "They're not good for you."

"I'll remember that the next time you want some," my father said.

"They're not good for you either, Stanley," Sally said. "It's not on your list of approved breakfast options."

"I hate smoothies," he bellowed. "The seeds get stuck in my teeth. I should reap vengeance on whoever invented seeds!"

Sally looked at me. "Yesterday he wanted to exact revenge on the creator of broccoli because it gave him gas."

"I would think that's a good thing," I said. "Save yourself the trouble of driving all the way to Asiago Street to fill up." With Princess Buttercup in tow, I hurried out the back door before Mount Stanley Fury could erupt.

CHAPTER TWO

IT WAS SUCH a beautiful day that I decided to walk into town. It was Saturday so I didn't *need* to be at the office, but I relished any excuse to be out of the house and away from my family. I also needed time to process the new addition to my mane. Why did it have to be snakes? Why couldn't it be extensions that made my hair look longer and fuller?

I found myself bypassing the road to my office and continuing toward the promenade and its sweeping view of the Chesapeake Bay. Sunlight glittered on the surface of the water, giving it a magical quality. Chipping Cheddar, Maryland was a hidden gem of a town that had been settled by English Puritans with surnames like Tasker, Danforth, and Cawdrey. Although they'd started as dairy farmers, many eventually turned to cheesemaking, and the street names and establishments reflected the town's unique history.

I was so enthralled by the picturesque view that I failed to notice when a car slowed alongside me.

"Hey, pretty lady."

I glanced over to see a familiar face hanging out of the window.

"Hey there, gorgeous." I scratched the pug behind the ear. "And hello to you, too, Chief Fox."

The chief grinned. "You should probably call me Sawyer now that we've exchanged spit."

"Probably best not to. I might slip." And if we intended to keep our relationship a secret—which I most certainly did—then Chief Fox he would remain.

"I don't know about you, but I wouldn't mind a slip of the tongue right now," the chief said, grinning.

My legs wobbled in response. It was hard not to hurl myself into the car and have my way with him. Thankfully, there was an innocent dog between us that prevented any impulsive moves. The pug had his own tongue issues. It seemed ten times too big for his small body. He seemed able to lick my hand no matter where I moved it on his head.

"Achilles," I said, laughing. His tongue tickled.

"Is it wrong that I'm getting jealous?" Chief Fox asked. "Are you busy? Want to go for a coffee?"

"I think I can manage one drink."

"Only because it's not a bar," he teased.

"Now you sound like my dad." I opened the door and placed Achilles on my lap.

"Okay, now I'm really jealous," the chief said, eyeing the dog.

"Down, boy," I said, although I quite enjoyed the reaction. Who wouldn't? The police chief who could pass for an underwear model was jealous of the dog sitting on my lap. I suddenly felt like the most desirable woman in the world, forgetting all about the snakes and my hideous nature.

"Did you walk from Munster Close?" he asked.

"I was in the mood for exercise," I said. "I needed to clear my head." Literally.

"I've been feeling that way too," he said. Chief Fox had recently discovered the existence of the supernatural world thanks to witnessing my death and subsequent resurrection. I'd told him the bare minimum, not wanting to overload him with information that was difficult for a human to process. He knew about the FBM, that I was a fury, and that my mother, Grandma, and Aunt Thora were witches, but I had no intention of ever telling him the nitty gritty. How could I tell the head of law enforcement that members of my evil family routinely broke the law?

"How are you feeling about everything I told you?" I asked.

"Confused about the Twilight Zone stuff, but not about you." He cast me a sidelong glance. "You're not having second thoughts, are you?"

"About you? Not at all."

"Good, I was worried that it was a reaction to being resurrected. Didn't want you to have regrets." He reached across the gearshift and curled his fingers around my hand. His skin was warm and comforting.

"How can I have regrets? We haven't done anything yet," I said.

"I like the 'yet' in that sentence," he said. "Gives me hope."

"I do think it's important that we keep it quiet," I said.

He lifted an eyebrow. "How quiet?"

I stroked the pug's back. "Quiet enough that no one knows. I worry about your safety," I said.

He chuckled. "Have you forgotten that I'm the chief of police?"

"You think that makes a difference? Guns generally don't work on supernaturals."

"Are you suggesting I'll become a target if our relationship becomes public knowledge?" He snagged a spot on the street right outside the coffee shop. I was relieved that he'd chosen The Daily Grind over Magic Beans. As wonderful as the coffee was at the newer shop, it was owned by Corinne

LeRoux, who'd recently dated the chief but bowed out gracefully when she realized he had feelings for me. Growing up, she and I had maintained a safe distance from each other thanks to the rivalry between our families, although it seemed that we were slowly building a bridge of our own. I was determined to split my precious caffeinated time between Magic Beans and The Daily Grind to show my support, but not yet. Corinne was too observant and she already knew the chief was interested in me.

"It's possible," I said. Although the statement was truthful, it wasn't the main reason.

He plucked Achilles from my lap and leashed him before getting out of the car. "So you want to date in secret?"

"I think it's the only option." I left the car and joined him at the door. "I told you before that dating you would violate FBI rules, but it's really the FBM's policy because of the whole supers mixing with humans thing. I don't want to risk my job by flaunting it."

The Daily Grind was packed, so we changed topics while we waited in line and ordered. We had to hover with our cups and hope that someone vacated a table. It seemed that every person that passed us couldn't resist stopping to pet Achilles, not that I blamed them. The adorable pug deserved every second of his local fame.

"Excuse me, Chief Fox. When will you be patrolling with dogs in need of adoption again?" a woman asked.

"Deputy Guthrie has been handling that recently," the chief said. "As soon as Achilles is through his chewing stage, I'll leave him home sometimes so I can show off more dogs from the shelter."

"You're an angel," she said, and pinched his cheek.

"Not really, but thanks," he said. Once she was out of earshot, he whispered in my ear, "Wait, do those exist?"

"I have an angel-human hybrid in my family," I said.

Tomas, Uncle Moyer's husband. Tomas was forever leaving a trail of his existence for humans to find, not because he was mischievous but because he was messy and absent-minded.

"Why don't we go to my office with our coffee?" Chief Fox suggested. "We can walk from here and we'll have more privacy."

My brow lifted. "Privacy for what?"

He grinned. "To talk, of course. I'm not planning to make you regret anything so soon."

Together we strolled down the sidewalk to the police station, chatting as though we'd known each other forever. One of the qualities I really liked about the chief was how at ease I felt in his presence. We could talk about the weather, traffic, or even the price of gas, and I would still find that conversation with him enjoyable.

Achilles seemed to stop every ten feet to mark his territory. The little pug seemed to have big ideas about his turf.

We breezed by the reception desk and headed for the solitude of his office. He wasted no time closing the door, setting down his cup, and snaking a hand around my waist.

"I want to get to know you, Eden Fury," he said. "Tell me everything."

"That's a tall order," I replied. "Why don't we narrow it down? Favorite color is blue. Favorite book is..." My mind went blank with his lips hovering tantalizingly close to mine.

"Tell me more about the supernatural world," he said. "You're a..."

"Fury."

"Is that why you're so angry all the time?" he asked.

I recoiled. "I'm not angry all the time."

"You can be very...commanding."

"That's not angry. That's just being forthright."

He chuckled. "That's not how we roll in the Midwest. I'm only familiar with passive aggressive behavior."

"I don't speak passive aggressive," I said. "I'm from the Mid-Atlantic. We only speak aggressive."

"I know," he said smoothly. "And I think I like it." He kissed me, hesitantly at first but then with more confidence. Heat burned through my body. I was fairly certain my toes actually curled.

Achilles barked and he broke off the kiss. "He wants a treat." The chief reached into his drawer and produced a morsel. Achilles sat dutifully and was rewarded. Once the treat was gone, the pug trotted over to the dog bed in the corner and curled into a ball.

I perched on the edge of the desk and the chief came to stand in front of me.

"If you're a fury, does that mean there are creatures like vampires and werewolves?" he asked.

"Yes on both counts."

His brow lifted. "Wow. Here in Chipping Cheddar?"

"Everywhere, but more here than many places because of the location."

He seemed slightly taken aback, as though he expected me to laugh and deny it. "Do I know any?"

"You know many." I wasn't comfortable outing anyone specifically, even to Chief Fox.

"And you hunt demons?"

"I don't care for the term hunting. I prefer tracking. I never aim to kill if I can help it. Only to return them to Otherworld where they belong."

"Like me. I only want to capture, not kill."

"You're from Iowa," I said. "You'd probably offer a demon a glass of pop before you tried to pop a cap in his butt."

"I'm not *that* nice," he said.

Oh, but he was. Deliciously nice. And it was my Kryptonite.

"So the FBI story is a ruse."

"Not completely. I did work for them. In fact, that was my dream job," I said. "I had no desire to work for the FBM."

He wrapped his arms around my waist. "Why not? Seems like you're tailor-made for it."

I couldn't explain without revealing too much about my family. I opted for vague. "I wanted to establish my independence. My family can be somewhat overbearing. I find it hard to be my authentic self around them."

"I understand." His hands warmed my waist. "So why did you leave the FBI then?"

I drew a deep breath. "I accidentally became a vampire and bit my partner."

He balked. "You what now?"

"I have something called siphoning powers where I can absorb another supernatural's power. Fergus and I were chasing a suspect. I didn't realize he was a vampire until it was too late."

"Fergus?"

"No, the suspect. I got to him first because I'm...well, I'm super-fast. Touching him triggered my siphoning ability and I went full vamp on poor Fergus when he caught up to me. He's fine, though," I added quickly. "Made a full recovery."

"But you didn't."

"No. I got shipped off here. Once the FBI knew the truth about me, they had no choice but to transfer me to the magical division. I'm too dangerous for the human side."

He shook his head. "I can't believe the FBI knows about this sort of thing and manages to keep it under wraps."

"I don't think everyone in the FBI knows," I said. "My partner didn't. Still doesn't."

"Ah, they have ways of making people forget? Like *Men in Black*?"

"Ours is magic rather than technology, but yes."

A loud voice burst through our conversation. "There's a

situation on Stilton Street. People are complaining. I think it's a code pink elephant."

"Pink elephant?" I queried. "Is that a potential crime or a Heffalump sighting?"

Chief Fox released me. "Sounds like a drunk and disorderly type deal. I'll check it out."

"Send Sean," I said. "Payback for his disorderly high school years."

"One of these days you'll have to tell me why the two of you hate each other so much," Chief Fox said.

"There's no story," I said. "He's a soulless ginger with garlic breath that curdles milk."

The chief hesitated. "Is he a…vampire?"

I laughed. "He's pale enough, but no. Just your average, annoying redhead." I jumped to my feet. "How about I come with you?"

He brightened. "I wouldn't mind the attractive company."

"What about Achilles?" I asked.

"I'll leave him at the office, just in case things get out of hand." He whistled and the pug trailed after us. He stopped beside the reception desk like he knew the drill.

The chief and I continued back to The Daily Grind for his car and his hand accidentally brushed against mine as he held open the door for me. I was pretty sure there were actual sparks.

"It's not going to stay a secret for long if we keep hanging out in public together," he remarked.

"Everyone knows I'm a federal agent," I said. "They'll assume it's for professional reasons."

"But the supernaturals in town know you're with the FBM?" he asked.

"They do. When I show my badge, humans see FBI and supers see FBM, except humans with the Sight. They can see the supernatural world without being one."

The chief shook his head and whistled. "That's got to be a tough line to walk."

"You'll have to ask Clara about it. She's one of them." Clara Riley was my best friend and an empath, which meant she had the Sight.

"No kidding." The chief turned on his lights and parked behind what appeared to be a party bus. It was taking up part of the lane and heads were poked out of every open window. As we got closer, I realized that this was less of a bachelor party and more of a wake. Everybody on the bus looked at least seventy years old.

Chief Fox and I exchanged glances. "This is not what I was expecting," he said.

"Hey, Chief!" An elderly man hung out of the bus wearing a helmet on his head that held two cans of beer.

Chief Fox swaggered up to the front of the bus and knocked on the door. The driver opened it with a sheepish smile.

"Welcome aboard," he said. "I'm Chip."

"What's the occasion, gentlemen?" The chief stepped onto the bus and I followed, remaining on the bottom step. I could see plenty from this vantage point.

"Hank is getting remarried," someone shouted. They all cheered and drank whatever was in their cups.

"This is a bachelor party bus?" I asked.

"We figured why the hell not?" Chip said. "We deserve to have as much fun as guys in their youth. I rented the bus and Aaron organized the beer. I'm not drinking, of course. Someone has to be the DD."

Aaron toasted us with a plastic cup and sloshed beer over the rim. "Hank deserves a party."

Everyone cheered again.

"Why are you parked in the middle of the road?" the chief asked.

"Bathroom break," Chip said. "One of the pitfalls of taking guys our age out to drink. Frequent stops."

"Not me," another man yelled. "I'm wearing a diaper!"

Chip laughed. "You always come prepared, Scott!"

"You're going to need to tone down the party," Chief Fox advised. "There've been complaints. How long do you intend to drive around?"

"We're stopping at a new bar every two hours or so," Chip said. "We've got plenty of life left in us yet."

A snore erupted from somewhere on the bus, indicating that at least one reveler had already had enough.

"Hank's first wife passed away two years ago," Chip said, lowering his voice. "Ovarian cancer. He never thought he'd fall in love at his age. He was so depressed, but Jana changed everything. We're just all really happy that he decided to get married again."

"And Jana doesn't mind this day of debauchery?" I asked.

"She said you only live once. She's very hip." He paused for a beat. "And she still has both of her original ones. Hips, I mean. Get it?" He laughed at his own joke and then sighed when neither of us reacted. "Geriatric humor is wasted on the young."

"I'm going to need you to calm things down a bit," the chief warned. "Not hanging out the windows. No parking in the road. You know, follow the rules of civilized society."

"Aye, aye, Captain Fox." Chip saluted him.

"Why don't you join us?" Aaron called. "You can be our good-looking wingman. We can't all be as lucky as Hank. Some of us are still searching for Ms. Right, the sequel."

"We have IV fluids at my house," Scott said. "Nobody will get dehydrated on my watch." He belched loudly.

"I'm on duty, but thanks," the chief said.

"We'll be ending the night at The Cheese Wheel later,"

Aaron said. "If you're off duty then, come see how many of us are left standing."

"I'll keep it in mind," the chief said. He turned and I left the bus to give him space to exit.

"Have fun storming the bars," I said.

An elderly man approached the bus, zipping up his pants. "It always takes longer than I think it will these days."

Chief Fox clapped him on the shoulder. "Drink plenty of water."

"Water is for chumps," the old man said, and boarded the bus.

CHAPTER THREE

"I CAN'T BELIEVE the chief knows," Clara said. We sat in a booth at Gouda Nuff, waiting for Sassy. She seemed perpetually late.

"It was kind of hard to avoid," I said. "He saw me die and then he saw me walking around a donut shop." I popped a French fry into my mouth.

"I mean, it must be a relief, right?" Clara asked. "No more secrets?"

"I wouldn't go that far," I said. "I've asked him to keep our dating a secret. I can't tell my family about us and I can't tell him about my family. That's a bridge too far."

Clara mulled it over. "Did you tell him about me?"

"I told him that you have the Sight, but that's it. I'm trying to avoid specifics because it's a slippery slope."

She smiled behind her glass of iced tea. "You just want him to be your slippery slope."

I groaned. "Sweet Hecate, don't make me think about it or I'll need to dump this iced tea on my head to cool off."

"Cool off from what?" Sassy slid into the booth beside Clara and immediately snagged a fry.

"Her hots for Chief Fox," Clara volunteered before I could stop her. My swift kick under the table was in vain because I caught my toe on the post instead and yelped.

"Can't blame you there," Sassy said. "If Tanner gave me a hall pass, that's the door I'd be knocking on."

"Oh, you need a hall pass for that, do you?" I asked. Sassafras 'Sassy' Persimmons was the last person I would have expected to befriend upon my return to Chipping Cheddar. She was the 'hussy' (Grandma's word) responsible for my most humiliating moment in high school—catching my boyfriend with another girl. Head cheerleader. Lead mean girl. Yet here we were sharing diner fries together and making jokes about her current and my former flame, Tanner Hughes.

"Well, Tanner travels so often. It isn't like he'd know," Sassy said.

"Sounds like a dare," Clara said. "How's everything between you two?"

Sassy heaved a deep sigh. "Fine. The same. He travels for work. We snatch a weekend here and there. The sex is great when we're together, but it seems so infrequent."

"No closer to a ring, huh?" I asked. The better I'd gotten to know Sassy, the more I realized that she was too good for him. Tanner had a god complex thanks to his mother's insistence that he walked on water and he'd never learned how to treat other people. He was only interested in how they treated him—correction—how they worshipped him. It had taken me a long time to see him for the narcissist he truly was.

Sassy chewed her lip. "We talked about it again the other night before he left for Newport News. He swore he was looking for the perfect solitaire. One that I'd be happy to wear for the rest of my life." She crunched on another fry.

"It's not about the ring, though. It's not even about the wedding. It's about the marriage. That's all I care about."

"Well, there's a bachelor party bus rolling around town today with a bunch of geriatrics," I said. "Don't give Tanner any ideas."

"Who would he invite?" Sassy asked. "He doesn't have any real friends. He doesn't seem to know how to cultivate meaningful relationships."

Uh oh. It sounded like there was more going on here than a failure to propose.

"What about you?" Clara asked. "Don't you consider yourself a meaningful relationship for him?"

"Yes, but I think a man should have more than his mother and girlfriend in his life, don't you? He rarely visits his grandmother in the home and she's the sweetest lady."

"Tanner always liked to be the big dog in a group," I said. "He didn't like to feel challenged or threatened by anyone, so I think that results in him keeping everyone at bay."

"I used to think he was so cool and aloof," Sassy said. "I mean, we know he's charming. He wouldn't be able to work in sales otherwise, but he's only interested in charming people who can earn him money. He only makes the effort if you can give him something in return."

I swallowed a mouthful of iced tea. "I hate to break it to you, Sassy, but he's always been like that. How do you think he ended up with you? You gave him what he wanted."

She glared at me. "Gee, thanks."

"I'm not trying to be mean," I said. "It's just a central part of his character. If it's not something you can accept about him, you may need to rethink your relationship."

"Maybe it's a blessing that he hasn't proposed," Clara added. "Maybe you don't really want to marry him. You've been waiting so long that you feel like you're too invested to walk away."

Sassy nibbled thoughtfully on another fry. "I have spent an awful lot of time working on our relationship. It can be exhausting at times. Are relationships supposed to be draining?"

Clara and I lowered our heads. Between us, we were hardly experts. "I don't think so," I finally said. "I don't find Chief Fox exhausting, not that I can say we're in a full-fledged relationship."

"You really can't say," Clara said directly to Sassy. "It's a secret."

Sassy's eyes widened. "Ooh, really? You're trusting me with a secret?"

"Why not?" I said. "If you tell anyone, I'll hex you."

She tossed her blond ponytail over her shoulder and laughed. "You're so funny, Eden." Bless Sassy's ignorant soul.

"Eden especially doesn't want her family to know," Clara added.

"Because they're so weird?" Sassy asked. "Except your brother. He's pretty cute."

"They have an issue with authority figures," I said vaguely. "They won't like that I'm dating a cop."

"But you're an FBI agent," Sassy said. "Does that mean they don't like you?"

Ha! Sassy was more insightful than she realized. "I'm family, so they make an exception." Sort of.

"An illicit affair," she said, her eyes shining. "I'm so glad I came to the diner."

"You cannot tell Tanner," I said. "Definitely not him."

"Are you only going to meet at his place?" Sassy asked. "How will this work logistically? If people see you out together, word will get back to your family."

"We haven't gotten that far," I said. "Right now we're taking it slowly."

"Oh, wow. That just gave me a nice visual." Sassy picked up a napkin to fan herself.

Hedwig's Theme from Harry Potter blasted from my phone. "Oh, crap! Neville." I snapped up the phone. "I'm sorry. I'll be right there. I'm in traffic."

Clara smothered a laugh as I tucked away the phone. "You're the worst liar."

"Is it an internet emergency?" Sassy asked. Like most humans in town, she believed that I worked in the cyber-crime unit of the FBI.

"Yes, those Russians are at it again," I said.

"You should write a story about her, Clara," Sassy said. "Her work is so interesting."

"I wish I had time to chat more about it, but I've got to go." I tossed money onto the table. "Not really the worst liar, am I?" I whispered to Clara and sailed out the door.

Neville and I stood near the river in Davenport Park, safely ensconced behind an invisibility shield. This was the only way we could conduct our training outside but still hidden. Even though the demons he conjured were simulations, they appeared remarkably real.

The wizard thumbed through a book, searching for new and exciting demons to challenge me so that I could progress to the next level. Grandma's Little Critters had nothing on the FBM.

"Are there any attractive demons you could simulate?" I asked.

Neville glanced up at me and pushed his glasses to the bridge of his nose. "Do you plan to defeat it or date it?"

"I've seen enough disgusting things today," I said.

Neville snapped the book closed and tucked it under his

arm. "Did you accidentally walk in on your grandmother in the bathroom again?"

"No, thank Hecate." I didn't want to tell him, but I knew I had to. As my assistant, Neville had the right to know. "You know how I get a new present when I use a lot of power?"

Neville clapped a hand over his mouth. Slowly the hand slid back to his side. "What is it? Can you breathe fire?"

I frowned. "I'm not a dragon."

"There is a definite history of furies breathing fire," he said. "Not all of them, naturally. Only a select few, but you..."

"Cannot breathe fire," I finished for him. "To be fair, that's probably preferable to the gift they dropped in my lap." Or on my head, to be accurate. "Read 'em and weep." I uncloaked my head.

"Son of a bench," he gasped. That was the closest Neville ever came to cursing.

"Aren't they just the prettiest things you've ever seen?" The snakes twisted around each other and hissed.

Neville approached with caution. "They seem to like the fresh air. Their tongues are flicking in and out like crazy."

"Don't get too close," I warned. "They're venomous." One slid down the back of my head and dipped beneath my shirt. I wriggled and tried not to laugh. "They also tickle."

The wizard stood with his mouth hanging open. "O wondrous reptilian woman."

"I'm not reptilian," I objected. "I have wings too."

"I suppose we shouldn't be surprised," Neville said. "Your resurrection was bound to induce a major trait."

I cloaked the snakes again and smoothed my hair. "I know, but I guess I was hoping to leap tall buildings or something."

"No need to leap when you can fly, Agent Fury." He wiggled his shoulders to indicate my hidden wings. "Well, now that you've shared this critical news, you may as well keep going." He returned to his place beside the oak tree.

"Keep going?" I echoed.

"Chief Fox," he said. He opened the book to the marked page. "The last time I saw the two of you together in Holes, you seemed on the cusp of declaring eternal love."

My face grew warm and I was relieved that Neville had his nose back in the book. "I think anyone who's tasted Paige's fritters feels that way."

"You know what I mean. What is the current status of your relationship with Chief Fox?"

I laughed. "Subtle. You didn't even look up from the book. How many times did you have to practice that in the mirror?"

Neville reluctantly met my gaze. "Only three. I believe I mastered it quite well."

"My relationship status with the chief is none of your concern."

"Oh, but it is, Agent Fury."

"This is personal," I insisted. "It has nothing to do with the FBM."

Neville offered a sympathetic look. "I'm not trying to be difficult, but you have to understand that the Federal Bureau of Magic is a secret organization. People like Chief Fox endanger the very fabric of our existence."

"His knowledge of the supernatural world means that he can help us, Neville," I said. "The FBM should be working with the local police."

"Does that mean that Deputy Guthrie should know as well?"

Ooh, he had me there. "I wouldn't go that far."

"Agent Fury, you know I have great respect for you, but you put us at risk as well as the chief by sharing such critical information."

I folded my arms. "So you're basically telling me that you're on my family's side."

Neville must have sensed that this was a dangerous declaration because he immediately averted his gaze. "Rest assured, most infernal of goddesses, I am on your team as always. That being said, we have a responsibility to the supernatural community. We can't let our personal feelings get in the way of that."

"What's your plan then? If I tell you that I'm dating him, are you going to report me to headquarters? File a report?"

Neville looked aggrieved. "I would never betray your trust."

"That settles it then. You don't ask any more questions about us and then you won't have to know anything. Plausible deniability." I pretended to dust off my hands. "Okay, Neville. Back to business." I much preferred to pretend I was back in the field than discuss personal matters. If I couldn't chase criminals on the streets of San Francisco, at least I could be active during these training sessions.

"Very well then." Neville set down the book and removed an item from his backpack from the zipped compartment. "I've been working on this new device that you might find useful. It's small enough to fit in your pocket." He produced a golden bag the size of a leaf and held it up for inspection.

"What am I supposed to do with that? Use it to transport my flea circus?"

"It's a bottomless bag," he said. "I made it as small as I possibly could. You can use it to carry and conceal much larger items."

I stared at the tiny bag. "How?"

"Allow me to demonstrate." He plucked a branch from the ground and proceeded to place it inside the bag, even though the branch was ten times the size.

"That's great, Neville. Next time I need wood for the fireplace, I'll be sure to bring your bag."

The wizard removed the branch and stuffed the bag into his pocket with a harrumph.

"I'm kidding," I said, immediately feeling guilty. "I'm sure the bag will be more useful than my snakes."

"Don't be too quick to dismiss it." Neville said. "Those snakes could prove very useful indeed."

"If I want to win the ugliest woman in Chipping Cheddar competition, then yes, extremely useful." I rolled up my sleeves. "Enough chatter. I have energy to burn."

"As you wish." He pulled a familiar drawstring bag from the front compartment of the backpack. "I won't name the demons. The only way you can defeat them is to identify what they are and how to fight them."

"Sounds good to me."

Neville pinched what looked like glitter and tossed it into the air. A skeletal creature morphed into view with eyes that burned red.

I angled my head for a better view. "Skeletor?"

"This is a demon from Otherworld, Agent Fury, not a villain from a cartoon."

"Right." I focused and thought back to the pages of notes I'd digested. "It's an ossium demon!"

"Excellent."

I performed a mental check of the possible methods I could use to defeat him and opted for brute strength.

"Bones were made to be broken," I said, once the ossium demon was reduced to a pile of bones on the ground. "Maybe you could fit those in your little bag and use them to make soup later."

Neville scowled and the bones disintegrated.

Four demons later and I was still raring to go. Neville, on the other hand, was now slumped against the oak tree.

"One more for the road?" I asked.

Neville released a sigh. "I underestimated your enthusiasm today, Agent Fury. I thought I'd be able to watch Midsomer Murders."

My phone started to sing a muffled version of *What Does The Fox Say?* "Wait. Hold that demon." I retrieved the phone from my pocket.

Neville looked at me askance. "Don't tell me that's your new ring tone for the chief."

I ignored him and answered the phone. "Hi."

"You busy?"

"Not really. I'm training and Neville's napping under a tree like a bored lumberjack."

Neville muttered under his breath.

"Want to meet me for a drink at The Cheese Wheel?" the chief asked. "I'm off duty now. We could happen to run into each other there. I've been practicing my look of pleasant surprise."

The suggestion was far too tempting to say no. "I'll meet you there in fifteen minutes."

"Fifteen minutes," Neville exploded. "I was ready to go an hour ago, but the chief calls and you're ready to drop everything."

"Will you be sweaty from all the practice?" Chief Fox asked hopefully.

I laughed. "I don't think you'd want me there if I were too sweaty."

"On the contrary, I want you anywhere."

I smiled into the phone and Neville groaned loudly. "Please tell him we are in the process of completing a serious training session."

"I need to go," I said. "Neville is getting restless."

"Tell that taskmaster that you deserve a personal life," Chief Fox said. "Hey, maybe he should come with you and we can find him a prospective girlfriend. That might chill him out."

"Good idea." I held my hand over the phone. "Neville, you're coming to the bar with me. We're going to hook you up."

"Hook me up?" Neville repeated. "You know I don't do drugs."

I pressed my lips together. "Not drugs. A lady friend. Come on, it's much better than that wizard forum you frequent."

"There's a wizard forum?" Chief Fox asked.

Neville shushed me. "You can't tell him everything."

"Relax. It's not like I told him your user name is…"

"Agent Fury!" he thundered.

"He's excited to join us," I told the chief. "See you soon."

CHAPTER FOUR

"I've never seen so many elderly gentlemen in one place in my life," Neville said. We'd seen the party bus in the parking lot, so I knew our gentlemen friends from earlier were here. Based on the current number, they seemed to have lost a couple revelers along the route though.

"I'm glad my mother isn't here," I said. "She'd be in a feeding frenzy."

"Doesn't she prefer them younger?" Neville asked.

"She prefers them male," I said. "Beyond that, I'm not sure." As I spoke, I spotted a woman in the shadows of the room, lingering beside the jukebox. Her red hair was a smidge too bright for her pale skin. "Speaking of feeding…"

Neville followed my gaze. "Vampire?"

"You bet." The vampire was too focused on her prey to notice me. She'd zeroed in on two of the older men at the bar. I recognized them from the bus—Scott and Hank, the groom-to-be. They had to be drunk beyond reason by now. They'd been drinking for hours.

The vampire sashayed across the room and positioned herself between the two men. I didn't like where this was going. Vampires in the human world generally behaved themselves. She had to know that biting someone didn't go unpunished. A violation could result in a one-way trip to Otherworld or, even worse, the death penalty.

"Why are you staring at them so intently?" Chief Fox appeared beside me, causing me to jump.

"Good evening, Chief Fox," Neville said.

The chief clapped a hand on the wizard's shoulder. "Neville, so happy you're here. We're going to make it our mission to find you a new lady friend tonight. Hey, is that why we're watching the redhead?"

"No," I said. "She's a vampire. I'm watching to make sure she doesn't overstep."

The chief blanched. "That woman is a vampire?"

"In the flesh," I said. "And she seems to be interested in their flesh. It worries me."

"You don't hunt them, right?" he said. "You're not a slayer like Buffy."

"Not a slayer," I agreed. "Excuse me, I'm going to have a word with her before things get out of hand." I didn't want to have to do paperwork on a Sunday because some vampire was an eager beaver.

I waltzed over to the trio and pushed my way in the middle. "Greetings and salutations."

"Hey, I remember you," Hank said. His eyes were glazed and his nose was tinged with red. "You were on our party bus earlier. Why'd you leave?"

"Because I'm not a seventy-five-year-old man," I said.

"Have you met Gloria?" Hank asked.

I flashed a bright smile. "I haven't had the pleasure." I stuck out my hand. "Hello, Gloria. Are you new in town?"

"I'm not local. I'm here visiting a friend."

"Thought so." I took out my badge and showed it to her.

"Listen, my name is Agent Fury and Chipping Cheddar is my territory. You feel me?"

Gloria's jaw tightened. "I think I do."

"You want her to feel you?" Scott asked. "I knew we came to the right bar." He high-fived Hank.

"These men are celebrating a friend's upcoming nuptials," I said. "They're not looking for any trouble."

"Neither am I," she said quietly.

"You work for the FBI," Hank said, sounding impressed. "My nephew works for them, too. He's in Virginia."

"It's a big organization," I said. "There are a lot of us."

Gloria slipped away without another word. I kept one eye trained on her while I continued to make small talk with the men.

"You scared her away," Scott said. "Thought I might get lucky."

"Trust me," I said. "It would have been quite the opposite." Gloria had disappeared down the hallway that led to the restrooms. I was pretty sure there was a back door too.

"I'm getting tired anyway," Scott said. "I think I should have Chip drive me home soon."

"Not me," Hank said. "I want to see the sun rise."

Scott shook his head. "And here I thought I was the nutty one. I've never seen you so alive. Jana's bringing out the crazy in you, pal. It's pretty awesome."

"Another pint of your finest ale," Hank called to the bartender.

"Will the party bus drop everyone home safely?" I asked.

"It better after the lengths we had to go to," Hank said.

"Great lengths for a party bus, huh?" I said. "Is it because of your ages?" I'd heard of companies not wanting to rent to younger men, but hadn't encountered the same discrimination against older men.

"Our first rental fell through, so we had to rent it from a

place in Baltimore," Scott explained. "It came off the boat yesterday. I think that's why Chip is behaving so responsibly tonight. He paid the deposit."

"He's usually the one passed out on the floor by ten," Hank added with a chuckle.

"There's actually a party bus boat?" I asked. That sounded dangerous.

"No, this company ships the busses from Mexico," Hank said. "The factory relocated there a few years ago from Detroit."

"What's the world coming to when we can't even get our party busses made in the USA?" Scott asked, quickly followed by a gaping yawn.

"Don't wait for the bus," I said. "Call a cab."

The other men from the bus still seemed to be enjoying themselves. They were dancing up a storm in the open section of the bar. I worried that the hospital would end up with an influx of bruised and broken hips tomorrow, as well as dehydrated bodies.

"Everything okay?" Chief Fox asked. He and Neville ventured over to check on me.

"Good," I said. "I should probably make sure my new friend isn't lurking outside, though."

"Should I come?" Chief Fox asked.

"Not for this," I said firmly. "This isn't your area."

"Maybe it should be."

"Absolutely not," Neville interjected. I could see the worry lines streaking across his forehead.

"Have a beer with Hank and Scott," I said. "I'll be right back." I threaded my way through the bodies and slipped down the hallway and out the back door. Naturally, the lone light fixture seemed to have a broken bulb.

"I know you're still here, Gloria," I said. Although I couldn't see her, I felt her presence.

Gloria stepped out of the shadows. "You again. Why are you stalking me?"

"Because you're stalking human veins. Can't let you do that. It's for your own good as well as theirs."

"You think your badge scares me?" Gloria seemed to have overcome her willingness to leave quietly.

"It's not my badge that should scare you."

She tilted her head, probably realizing that she couldn't place me. Not all supernaturals could. I was too rare a beast. "What are you?" she asked.

I revealed myself slowly, unfurling my wings and letting the crown of snakes hiss and coil on my head. Gloria scampered backward at the sight of me.

"I don't want any trouble," she said. "I only wanted a bite to eat."

"Then go to a blood bank," I said. "Buy a fizzy blood orange. You know you can't snack on humans. The penalty isn't worth it."

Gloria's expression became anguished. "I normally don't get cravings. I don't know why I felt so hungry for the real deal tonight."

"Are you really visiting a friend?" I asked. One of the snakes slithered down to rest in my cleavage and I tried to nonchalantly shift it away without ruining my tough appearance.

"Yes, that's true," Gloria said. "Patti didn't feel like coming out. We spent the day in town. I'd seen the party bus earlier today, so when I saw it parked here, I decided to come inside."

"And then you decided to linger out here, waiting for a potential victim to stagger out here all drunk and disorderly so you could justify your attack."

Gloria put her hands on her hips. "What about you with your venomous hat?"

"It's not a hat," I said tersely. "And I don't attack people with them. I protect people. That's part of my job."

"You're some kind of freakish superhero? Did you get bit by a radioactive snake?" She frowned. "No, that doesn't explain the wings."

"I'm a fury," I practically shouted. "Now go back to your friend's house and stop thinking about using your fangs as a crazy straw."

Gloria's focus returned to my head. She seemed more concerned with the snakes than the wings. "I've never seen a fury before. I thought you were extinct."

"Consider it a gift. We specialize in punishment."

Gloria's eyes widened slightly. "I'm pretty beat. I think I'll be going now."

"Good plan." I watched as she ran around the corner of the building and blended with the shadows.

"Eden?"

Great balls of fury. I quickly cloaked my traits and turned toward the sound of his voice. "Chief?"

"Are you okay out here?" He stepped outside, his face illuminated by the moonlight. That chin dimple alone was enough to sweep me off my feet, forget about the handsome face and rock-solid body.

"I'm fine, thanks." I met him at the door. "Gloria seemed to be having an issue. Hopefully I helped get her back on track."

"Why don't you kill them?" he asked.

"Vampires?"

He nodded. "Why not stake them and eliminate the threat entirely?"

"Because the vampires living in this world generally want to live a more human existence. They're happy to drink their bottled blood and spend their weekends trying out new cookie recipes." Like my stepmom, Sally.

"They're not all predators?"

"No, definitely not."

"Do you think I know any vampires back in Iowa?" he mused.

"I'd bet good money on it."

He tipped his head, thinking. "Mr. Thornton could have been one. My old baseball coach."

"What makes you think that?" It was unlikely Chief Fox would be able to identify them so quickly. It took most humans years of exposure and practice to get it right.

"He loved a good Bloody Mary."

I laughed. "That's because he probably loved too much beer the night before."

The chief clasped my hands in his. "How about we love too much beer right now? Give us an excuse to wrap our arms around each other later, prop each other up."

I slid an arm across his broad shoulders. "Who needs an excuse?"

The next morning, I stumbled downstairs from the attic. I was desperate to get rid of the thin layer of film that had formed over my teeth in the night, probably because I forgot to brush them after I came home. My dentist would not be pleased.

"No playing fast and loose with dental hygiene," he would say, completely serious. "You've got to commit to those teeth. They're the only real set you'll get."

"Is that Eden or a Sasquatch?" Grandma asked from the table. "I can't see past the tangled hair."

I tugged the knotted strands off my face. "Your granddaughter. Sasquatches are too scared to come here."

My mother and Aunt Thora were also at the table. The smell of freshly baked banana muffins pulled me into their sphere against my better judgment. I reached for a muffin and nobody smacked my hand away. A good start to the day.

"You were home late last night," my mother said. "I was up reading and heard the door well past one o'clock."

"I would think you'd award her a gold star for that," Grandma said. "She's finally taking after you."

I focused on my mother. "Okay, I don't know what you were actually doing at one in the morning, but we both know it wasn't reading."

My mother shifted uncomfortably in her chair. "Fine. I was scrolling through Instagram."

"That's more like it," I said. "Reading involves words."

"So do hexes," my mother said in her warning tone.

I ignored her and went to the stovetop. "Coffee?"

"Do we look like amateurs to you?" Grandma asked.

I checked the pot. There was enough left for half a cup. It would have to do because I was desperate.

"There was an incident at The Cheese Wheel last night," I said. "That's why I was out late."

"Demonic activity at the bar?" My mother leaned forward intently. "Tell me more."

"It wasn't a demon. A bunch of aging bachelors acting up caught the attention of an opportunistic vampire."

My mother's eyelashes fluttered. "Why didn't you call me? I would have come to tame those savage beasts."

"The bachelors weren't the problem, Beatrice," Grandma said. "It was the bloodsucker hoping for a happy ending."

"You mean a Happy Meal," my mother said. "A happy ending is something else. Trust me, I know."

I cringed. "There was no need for civilian involvement. Chief Fox was there." I caught the look that passed between the women at the table.

"So you were at the bar late last night with Chief Fox?" my mother asked.

"I wasn't *with* Chief Fox," I said. "We both happened to be there."

"Who were you with?" Aunt Thora asked.

"I promised Neville I'd try to find him a girlfriend."

My mother flicked a dismissive finger. "Oh, that little wizard isn't going to date anyone. He's too sweet on you."

"Neville is not sweet on me," I insisted. "He has a professional respect for me. There's a difference."

"Why would the chief of police get involved in a vampire issue?" Grandma asked. "It's not like he knows about them."

I gulped. "He didn't know," I lied. "He thought the men were being propositioned by a hooker. We'd met them earlier in the day on a party bus and knew they were wasted..." Oops.

"We," my mother repeated. "You and Chief Fox?"

Keeping our relationship secret was going to be tougher than I thought, especially while I still lived in the house. "I happened to be passing by when he was called to the scene," I said. "The party bus was illegally parked. Anyway, it doesn't matter. That's why I was out late."

I obviously wasn't convincing enough because my mother said, "I see how he looks at you. He is off limits."

"I told you Neville has a healthy respect..."

She cut me off. "I'm not talking about the little wizard and you know it."

"Eden's no better," Grandma added. "She looks at him the way Beatrice looks at the Buxmont sextuplets."

"Which one?" I asked.

"All of them," Grandma replied.

A dreamy look crossed my mother's face. "Imagine having all of them at the same time."

"Chief Fox is so nice and handsome," Aunt Thora said. "Don't you think you're rushing to judgment? Eden could do much worse."

"That's true," Grandma said. "She could still be with that awful Tanner Hughes."

My mother groaned. "Don't even say that deplorable human's name."

"What a loser," Grandma agreed.

"He's an attractive young man," Aunt Thora said. "I can understand the appeal."

"I don't think the chief is a good idea and that's that," my mother said. She seemed determined to hammer this point home.

"I didn't think you and Stanley were such a good idea either," Grandma said. "And you can see how much influence I had there."

My mother's head swiveled toward her. "You literally tied me to the rafters and threatened to starve me until I broke up with him."

Grandma shrugged. "Look on the bright side, you lost ten pounds that month. You never looked better."

My mother appeared thoughtful. "I haven't thought about being tied up for weight loss. I've only been using it for..."

I held up a hand. "Empty stomach."

"Your mother's right, though," Grandma said. "Chief Fox is a liability we can't afford."

"He's the chief of police," I said. "I can hardly avoid him."

"I'm not saying to avoid him," Grandma replied. "I'm saying not to get too close."

"Fine," I said, lying through my teeth. "I'll keep it professional."

"See?" my mother said. "I told you Eden would do the right thing. She always does."

"Normally it's a drag but, in this instance, I'm good with it," Grandma said.

Princess Buttercup materialized in the kitchen, her ears alert. Someone was here.

"Hello, anybody home?" Verity called. She rounded the corner with my nephew on her hip. "I've already dropped off Olivia at a friend's. I'm sorry to dump and run, but I have a full workload today."

"But it's Sunday," my mother objected.

"We've had a sudden uptick in emergencies," Verity said. "When it's like this, I'm not about to send everyone to the ER."

"Is something going around?" I asked.

"Nothing connected," Verity said. "Arthritis. Nerve pain. Digestive issues. Migraines. It was relatively quiet and then —bam!"

"Bam!" Ryan echoed.

My mother scooped the toddler out of his mother's arms and nuzzled him. "There's my precious evildoer. Who's my little devil?"

Ryan bonked her on the nose with his small fist.

"I'll be working late, but Anton will pick him up before dinner," Verity said.

"He's still away?" my mother asked.

"Comes back tonight, thank the gods," Verity said. "I wish he didn't take these side jobs."

I bet Verity had no idea that my brother's side jobs were vengeance-related. He'd told me that he'd basically given up that line of work, but they'd just had major renovations done on their house. Everybody was a hypocrite when it came to money, it seemed.

"Anton and the kids might as well stay for dinner if the lady of the house won't be there to feed her family," my mother said.

Oh boy.

Verity bristled. "Anton is more than capable of feeding himself and the children."

"I know, but he's been working so hard and he'll have just gotten home. He shouldn't have to," my mother said.

I could see each vein in Verity's usually smooth head rise to the surface. "I'll let you work that out with Anton," the healer said through gritted teeth.

My mother smacked her lips all over Ryan's face and he laughed and tried to squirm out of her arms. Beatrice Fury was a difficult mother and mother-in-law, but I couldn't argue with her role as grandmother.

"Have a good day, Verity," I said.

"Thanks." My sister-in-law wisely escaped the house before my mother could say something else to annoy her.

My mother placed Ryan on the stool at the island and sliced a muffin in quarters for him. "While I'm thinking about it, what are you wearing to Myrtle's funeral?" Myrtle Blackwood was an elderly witch who'd died peacefully in her sleep. Although she didn't have a local coven, she'd been friendly enough with the other witches in town that they'd promised to host her funeral services.

"Your daughter-in-law was just here and your mind goes to a funeral?" I asked. "Go figure."

"Black," Grandma said. "What did you think I'd wear? A rainbow tutu with sparkling tights?"

"Myrtle was such a character though," my mother said. "A black dress seems too formal for her funeral."

"I'm a character. What would you wear to mine?" Grandma asked.

My mother beamed, the answer sliding effortlessly from her lips. "That flattering crimson dress with a black hat and red spiked heels so I can dance on your grave."

Grandma scowled. "I don't like how much thought you've already given this."

"I'll be under the spotlight," my mother said. "I'm your

daughter. The eyes of all the mourners will be on me and my hip-hugging dress." She ran her hands down her sides, seeming to picture it. "How many men do you think we should invite?"

Grandma looked at me in exasperation. "She's already planning it."

"You started it," I said.

Grandma shifted back to my mother. "What would you say?" she prompted.

My mother blinked. "Say? I suppose I'd tell them we've suffered a tragic loss and that they were more than welcome to comfort me..."

"The eulogy, Beatrice," Grandma snapped. "What would you say about me?"

My mother hesitated. I rarely saw her deer-in-the-headlights expression, but I had a full view of it now.

"I would say my sister was a formidable witch that lived life on her own terms," Aunt Thora said, coming to the table with a fresh cup of tea. A wedge of fresh lemon teetered on the edge of the cup.

Grandma snorted. "What makes you think you'll still be around to attend my funeral?"

Aunt Thora sat beside her. "I upset far fewer supernaturals."

"You think a supernatural can put me in the ground?" She cackled. "I'd like to see one try."

"I can put you in the ground," my mother said evenly. "Wouldn't be the first time either."

Ryan smashed a piece of muffin with his fist and did his best impression of a cackle.

I cleared my throat. "I would say that you were a fine example of a black magic witch."

"A fine example?" Grandma replied. "What—I'm on display in a museum?"

"No, you're in a textbook," my mother said with a snicker.

"You'd be the main speaker, Mom," I said. If she was going to mock me, then I had no trouble throwing her under the bus. "What would you say about Grandma?"

My mother glared at me before plastering on a smile for Grandma. "Naturally, I would say that my mother was the guiding force in my life and that she possessed more power in her pinky than most witches possessed in their entire coven." She watched Grandma expectantly, waiting for her approval.

"I think you can do better," Grandma said.

My mother groaned. "What's wrong with that?"

"It's boring," Grandma said.

"It is kind of boring," I agreed.

My mother smoothed back her hair. "Fine. Then what would you like me to say?"

Grandma rubbed the wart on her chin. "I want you to promise to avenge my death."

"But what if you die of natural causes or an accident?" I asked.

Grandma smiled. "Who cares? It'll scare the daylights out of everybody in the room. They'll wonder who's responsible."

"I won't do that," my mother said. "I want to seem approachable to our guests. Vulnerable even."

Grandma pointed a menacing finger at her. "Then do me a favor and don't give the eulogy at my funeral. Let Eden do it."

Uh oh. "I don't want to give any eulogies." I planned to linger by the snack table and grieve in solitude—with the chips bowl.

My mother didn't seem to care that I'd objected to the role. She wanted to bury me anyway. "You think Miss Pride and Prejudice can deliver a eulogy befitting a dark witch of your stature?"

I blinked. "Miss Pride and Prejudice? Have I won some kind of literary beauty pageant?"

"At least she won't make my funeral about her because she's not a raging narcissist," Grandma said.

"How about I just bury you with your phone and the Little Critters app and call it a day?" my mother asked. "No service necessary."

CHAPTER FIVE

I PARKED in the lot at Barre None and headed inside to meet Clara and Sassy for a Sunday session. Between last night and this morning, I was ready to dive into relaxation mode. If I stretched a few muscles in the process, even better.

Clara and Sassy were already on their mats, chatting quietly. I didn't recognize the other people in the class. Although yoga wasn't really my thing, I was trying to adopt the lifestyle. I figured it couldn't hurt to be more chill.

"Good morning," I said. I unrolled a mat next to Clara and dropped onto my bottom. "What are we talking about?"

"Clara's newspaper assignment," Sassy said. "Such a sad story."

"At least it's a story," I said. All the best assignments were usually given to the undeserving Gasper Cawdrey.

"It's not that sad," Clara said. "People die every day. It's a fact of life."

"Do you mean Myrtle Blackwood?" I asked. Death was often sad, but it was hard to pity a ninety-five-year-old witch who'd lived a full life.

Clara looked at me. "Who's that? I'm writing an article about Dayna Butters."

"I don't know her," I said.

"She died of cancer and her mom was able to raise enough money for her funeral through lemonade stands and bake sales," Sassy said. "Isn't that amazing?"

"How old was Dayna?" I asked.

"Ten," Clara said.

"Oh, wow," I breathed. I wasn't expecting such a serious topic this early on a Sunday morning. I would have preferred an inane conversation about the best burger in Chipping Cheddar.

"Clara is going to interview her mom," Sassy said.

I cut a glance at Clara. "Are you going to be okay?" As an empath, Clara often found herself overwhelmed by emotions, especially if she touched someone in turmoil.

Clara wore a stoic expression. "I'll be fine. I'm a professional. Tough topics are part of the job."

"If you say so." I copied her position and tried to push my forehead toward my knees. How about flexibility for a fury trait? I'd have to put in a request to the Powers-That-Be, not that anyone was listening. If they were, I wouldn't be a fury at all.

Sassy observed my struggle to maintain the position. "You know, Eden. I'd be happy to practice with you. I don't think coming here once a week is enough."

"What's wrong with this?" I asked, not wanting to admit defeat. I wiggled my fingers in a vain effort to reach my toes.

"What's not wrong with it?" Clara asked.

"Where's Mrs. Marr?" I asked. The former secretary for my high school principal had been the instructor the last time I was here.

"I heard someone say she was too hungover to come in," Clara said.

"Mrs. Marr?" I asked, aghast.

"I know," Sassy said. "I had the same response." She shrugged. "I guess when you get to be her age, it's YOLO and all that."

"Then who's leading the class?" I asked.

A familiar voice set my teeth on edge. "Good morning, yogis. I've been asked to sub for Francine today. Sorry for the last-minute change."

Gale Hughes, Tanner's mother, waltzed to the front of the room and admired herself in the multiple mirrors before sinking onto a mat. Sassy looked as stunned as the rest of us.

"Oh, hello, Sassy," she said. "I didn't realize you were here. I hope you made my son a healthy breakfast before you indulged in 'me time.'"

Sassy flinched. "Tanner isn't back from Newport News until tonight."

Mrs. Hughes seemed momentarily confused. "Of course. I'd forgotten." She glowered when she spotted me in the group. "Still keeping mixed company, I see."

Sassy lifted her chin. "Eden's my friend, Gale. Tanner doesn't have a problem with it, so I don't see why you should."

"Tanner doesn't have a problem with it because he's holding out for a threesome," Clara pointed out.

"And they'd be lucky to have the experience," Mrs. Hughes said.

Now that was some motherly devotion right there.

Mrs. Hughes snapped her fingers. "All right, everyone. If you want those bodies limber, you need to follow my lead."

I watched in amazement as she flipped her legs over her head and formed an arch. I was beginning to understand why Mrs. Hughes always had a boyfriend despite her abrasive personality.

Sassy and most of the class followed suit. Clara and I exchanged glances.

"I'll spot you," I offered.

"No, I can do it," Clara said. "I just don't want to do anything that woman says."

"Same." I paused. "Okay, not same. I can't do it, but even if I could, I wouldn't want to." I waited for Clara to crack a smile, but she remained expressionless.

"I'm not going to get anything out of this class without Mrs. Marr." Clara rolled up her mat. "I'll see you two later."

I was torn between following Clara and keeping Sassy company. It seemed rude to just walk out. Clara was usually more willing to suck it up when someone else's feelings were involved.

"You can go if you want," Sassy whispered. Her blond ponytail dragged across the floor. "I totally understand."

"I see that not everyone here is flexible," Mrs. Hughes said, changing position. "I guess that's why you lost your grip on a worthy man."

I winced. "Sorry, Sassy. I hate to abandon you."

"I'll be fine," she said. "Save yourself."

I rolled up my mat and returned it to the far wall. I didn't miss her smug expression when she saw me prepare to leave. I was so tempted to give Tanner's mom a good look at my new crown, but there was no way to manage it without showing the rest of the class too. Stupid mirrors.

As I headed for the door, she switched to downward-facing dog, her bottom high in the air. In that moment, I remembered a basic spell I'd used on Sean Guthrie in high school, after he'd told Tanner that dating me was ruining Tanner's cool reputation. I wiggled my finger and whispered an incantation. I heard the satisfying sound of tearing fabric and a collective gasp. That was enough for me. I smiled to myself and slipped out the door.

. . .

"Back from yoga so soon?" Aunt Thora asked. She was placing homemade cookies into a Tupperware container.

"There was an unexpected setback." I filled a glass with water and gulped it down.

"I need to go see Ted at the lighthouse," Aunt Thora said.

"Need? Is there a problem?"

"He's upset. You know how he gets when he's not at peace with himself," she said.

In my underrated opinion, Ted O'Neill wasn't 'at peace with himself' most of the time. The guy kept a mannequin for company in the lighthouse. Then again, Aunt Thora had a soft spot for him and he was the brother of the former chief, Mick O'Neill, so I tended not to judge him too harshly.

"Do you know why?" I asked.

"He wouldn't say, so that's what I'm going to find out," Aunt Thora said. "I baked him a batch of oatmeal cookies and I'm bringing a thermos of homemade lemonade. I thought they might cheer him up."

"You're so sweet." I didn't know how my great-aunt managed to maintain her aura of goodness in this house of murk. I long suspected she was the most powerful witch of all.

"Would you like to join me?" she asked. "I'm sure Ted would love the extra company. He gets so lonely in that lighthouse."

I hesitated. As much as I loved Aunt Thora, the thought of socializing with Ted and his mannequin in the confined space of the lighthouse wasn't exactly appealing.

"You can have as many cookies as you'd like," she added.

Ooh, she knew how to manipulate me, that wicked witch. "Sold."

I didn't bother to change. Ted would be too busy entertaining his mannequin to notice my yoga pants and Basic Witch T-shirt.

We drove across town with Aunt Thora taking a strange zigzag path instead of the road that ran parallel to the water. I ignored the haphazard route and gazed out the window instead. The sky was the kind of flat blue that looked more like a ceiling than the start of the final frontier.

"Have you given any thought to your eulogy?" I asked.

Aunt Thora kept her eyes on the road. "I'm not giving a eulogy for Myrtle. We were friendly, but not friends, if you know what I mean."

"I'm not talking about Myrtle. I mean what you'd want people to say about you."

Aunt Thora bit back a smile. "I don't much mind what people say about me, especially when I'm dead."

"Now you sound like Grandma." But a nicer, more polite version.

"Oh, don't be fooled. Your grandmother cares what others would say. She just hides it better than most." Aunt Thora parked as close as she could to the lighthouse. It was best to minimize the steps between the car and the lighthouse. The winding staircase to the top was brutal enough.

"If she cares so much, then she might want to reconsider how she behaves," I said. "Cutting in front of the line at the supermarket doesn't endear you to the masses."

"She could choose to hex them all and still get to the front of the line," Aunt Thora pointed out. "Shouldn't she get credit for showing restraint?"

"It's not like people know what she's capable of," I said. "To them, she's an ornery old woman with entitlement issues."

"She is that," Aunt Thora said with a gentle laugh.

We climbed the steps to the lighthouse and I took my time so as not to leave Aunt Thora in the dust. We made it to the top to find Ted seated at a small square table with the mannequin across from him. There was a chess board set up between them.

"We come bearing gifts," Aunt Thora said. She produced the lemonade and the cookies and Ted's clouded expression evaporated. Who needed magic when you had baked goods?

"Oatmeal?" he asked.

"Of course," Aunt Thora said. "I know what you like." She placed a cookie on a napkin and gave it to him.

"Thank you, Thora. You're always so thoughtful." He inhaled the aroma before taking a bite. "Delicious. Won't you have one, Eden?"

"You don't have to ask me twice." I snatched a cookie from the container.

Aunt Thora looked at the mannequin. "Hello Mildred. You don't mind if I steal your seat, do you?" She shifted it aside and sat across from Ted. "Tell me what's gotten you so low."

"It's Father Kevin," Ted said. "He made an announcement at the end of services this morning."

"What kind of announcement?" Aunt Thora pressed.

"He's leaving," Ted said. "He's been in charge of our flock for so many years. I can't imagine going to services without him."

"He's going to another parish?" I asked. It was hard to put on a sympathetic face when the taste of Aunt Thora's home-made cookie lingered on my tongue. It was a transcendental experience.

"No, much worse," Ted said. "He's decided to leave the church. Says he doesn't believe anymore."

I nearly choked on my cookie. "The priest is leaving because he's lost faith?" And he thought it was good idea to announce it to the whole parish? Yikes.

Ted flicked one of the chess pieces with his finger,

knocking it over. “If my own priest doesn’t believe anymore, where does that leave me?”

“I’m so sorry to hear that,” Aunt Thora said. She gave his hand an affectionate squeeze. “More lemonade?”

“Don’t mind if I do,” he said.

“I can’t imagine the parishioners reacted very well to his announcement,” I said.

Ted shook his head sadly. “The whole church was in chaos. Babies were crying.” He paused. “Well, babies are always crying in church. It seemed like the world was collapsing in front of our eyes. The end of days.”

“That’s a bit dramatic, don’t you think?” Aunt Thora asked. She had a way of saying the thing you were thinking without sounding judgmental or bitchy. It was a talent.

“Did he say why?” I asked. “Give any reason at all?” Maybe he’d fallen in love. It happened. I knew of a priest and a nun in San Francisco who fell in love and left the church to get married. They went on to have three children and were still together. Fergus was one of the children. It was a story he tended to trot out after a few beers. He seemed both embarrassed and proud. He knew it had been a difficult decision for them, but they had no regrets.

Ted bit into his cookie and chewed mechanically. “Said that the universe was an uncaring and unfeeling place. That the bad were never adequately punished and the good were punished more than their fair share, but there was nothing he could do so he may as well give up. He wanted to care, but he just didn’t anymore.”

“Sounds more like a midlife crisis,” Aunt Thora said.

“Priests aren’t supposed to have midlife crises,” Ted objected. “They’re men of the cloth.”

“I can understand why this is upsetting for you,” I said.

Ted nodded absently as he nibbled on the cookie. “I want to stay here until he believes again.”

"Don't do that," Aunt Thora said. "You have to take care of yourself, Ted. You can't let Father Kevin's crisis have a negative impact on you."

"How can it not?" he shot back. "I've been listening to him, believing him, for years." He shook his head. "I feel so confused."

"I completely understand," Aunt Thora said. "Would you like to play chess? Might help take your mind off it."

Ted managed a smile. "You always know how to cheer me up. You're the best, Thora."

I went for a walk along the promenade and let the two of them play in private. I knew if I were trying to cheer up the chief, I wouldn't want an audience. Aunt Thora texted me when she was finished and I returned to the base of the lighthouse.

"I think you need to look into this," Aunt Thora said, on the drive back to Munster Close.

"Look into what?"

"Father Kevin. There might be magic afoot."

I laughed. "You think it's magic that caused a priest to lose faith rather than the garbage fire of a world we live in? I'm sure Father Kevin has access to the internet. He sees what's going on out there."

Aunt Thora was silent for a beat. "Please, Eden. A decision like this can have a ripple effect on people. Look at Ted. Do you think he's the only one feeling despondent over this?"

No, probably not. "I don't see how I can change that."

"Do your job," Aunt Thora urged. "Investigate." She tapped her fingers on the steering wheel. "There's another batch of cookies in it if you do."

"Bribing a federal agent, Aunt Thora? Whatever next?" I sighed. "Fine. I'll talk to Father Kevin and see if anything supernatural is going on."

"Thank you."

We all had a price. Apparently mine was baked goods. I stared out the window at the passing scenery of our picturesque little town. I would have stayed in Chipping Cheddar quite happily if I hadn't been trying to escape my family.

"How do you manage?" I asked.

Aunt Thora glanced at me. "Manage what?"

"To live here with them," I said.

My great-aunt understood. "Don't give me too much credit, Eden. I wasn't always this mellow."

I didn't know the details of Aunt Thora's younger, more evil life and it was probably best to keep it that way. Her late husband Cyrus had been an excessus demon, one that encourages excessive behavior like drinking, smoking, gambling. Needless to say, they weren't exactly known for their cuddly and sweet demeanors.

"You're like the Great Dane of witches," I announced. "That's what I'd say at your funeral."

Aunt Thora glanced at me. "Pardon me?"

"A gentle giant in the world of black magic," I said.

"I like Great Danes." She turned the car down our street and I noticed her lips curve into a vague smile. "That'll do."

CHAPTER SIX

I KNOCKED on the door of a modest single-story house across the street from the church. According to Aunt Thora, the house was called a rectory and belonged to the church. The front door must not have been fully latched because it cracked open.

"Father Kevin?" I called.

There was no response. I called his name again. When there was no reply, I started to worry about the priest's state of mind. What if his crisis of faith was worse than we thought? I decided to play the agent card. I pulled out my badge and entered the house.

"Father Kevin, this is Agent Eden Fury from the FBI," I said loudly. I took another cautious step inside. The living room was quiet and devoid of personal items. As I strained to listen, I heard voices coming from down the hallway. Was Father Kevin entertaining guests—in his bedroom?

My body tingled with energy as I made my way past each open door. Bathroom. Guest bedroom. The master bedroom door was ajar.

"Father Kevin," I yelled. "I'm coming in." I nudged the

door open with my foot. The priest was on the bed in a plaid pajama set, snacking on a bowl of popcorn while he watched television. His gaze flicked to me and then back to the screen. I stepped further into the room to see which show had transfixed him.

"Bravo?" I blurted. I wasn't sure why I was so shocked. It wasn't as though he'd tuned into the Kardashians.

Father Kevin kept his gaze locked on the screen, where a slender, well-dressed housewife was screaming at a table of women. Mascara streaked down her angular cheeks. She seemed to be having some sort of breakdown. After a moment of watching this dramatic scene, I snapped back to actual reality and focused on Father Kevin.

"Can we talk, Father Kevin?"

"I'm not listening to confessions anymore," he said. His speech almost sounded slurred.

"I'm not here to confess." Even a priest didn't have that much time on his hands for my list of confessions. "I'm here to talk about you."

His brow shot up. "What about me?"

"I'm standing in your bedroom in the middle of the day while you lay in pajamas and watch reality television with a bowl of popcorn. I think it's obvious."

His sigh was so deep that it seemed to rattle his chest. He set aside the bowl of popcorn and paused the show. "I've lost faith."

"So I gathered." I gestured to the corner of the bed. "Mind if I sit?" I didn't like towering over him like it was an interrogation. It made me uncomfortable. Not sure why sitting on the priest's bed made me more comfortable, but whatever.

He shrugged, so I sat. "I don't know what to do next. I should probably shower."

Now that he mentioned it, there was a certain stench.

"What happened, Father? You woke up one morning and realized that you no longer believed?"

"Basically," he said. "I'd spent a beautiful day at the marina on Friday with two of my parishioners, Judy and Paul Masterson. They own a boat and invited me to join them. I felt God's blessings that whole day. Even the sunset was glorious." He smiled sadly at the memory. "I woke up yesterday with a deep sense of ennui. I tried to go through the motions, but I couldn't live with the hypocrisy."

"Have you noticed anything unusual?" I asked. "For example, did you eat anything you wouldn't normally eat?" Maybe the Mastersons were involved in black magic and wanted to oust the priest for some reason. I'd have to check them out.

Father Kevin seemed to really see me for the first time. "Did I hear you say you're FBI?"

"That's right. I work with Chief Fox sometimes." That was a name he'd be comfortable with.

"Oh, okay." Father Kevin appeared unconcerned. I could have been the devil sitting there with horns and a pitchfork and he would've carried on with his popcorn and television. "I don't remember what we ate. Judy packed us a lunch. Nothing fancy. I drank water. The sun was warm, I remember that. I had to apply sunscreen twice."

"That's your pale Irish skin," I said.

"Lots of us in Chipping Cheddar. Did you know Chief O'Neill?" he asked.

"I did. He was friends with my father. They used to golf together."

Father Kevin nodded. "Mick enjoyed a good golf game. Who's your father?"

"Stanley Fury," I said.

The priest's brow furrowed. "Fury, yes. That name rings a bell."

Probably because it was on the naughty list of all religions.

"Why are you thinking about Chief O'Neill?" I asked. I didn't like that he seemed to be steering the conversation toward death. A midlife crisis due to possible magic was one thing. Serious depression was one I wasn't equipped to deal with.

"It just seemed so unfair," Father Kevin said. "Mick was a good, devout man."

"Mick was a cop. He knew the risks," I said. "He wouldn't want anyone to pity him." And if his ghost were still around, I would have gotten a direct quote to support that statement.

Father Kevin's eyes glazed over. "At first I thought I was being punished for enjoying myself too much the day before," he said. "That I'd overstepped, but I began to realize that no one was punishing me because no one was there. We're alone and nothing matters. Why bother to care?" He plucked a kernel from the bowl and popped it into his mouth. "I haven't had popcorn since I was a boy. It seemed too sinful because I enjoyed it so much, so I gave it up."

It still seemed like some kind of emotional breakdown to me, but I continued questioning him for Aunt Thora's sake. "Can you think of anything out of the ordinary that happened before you started feeling…despondent?"

"I've been listening to Bohemian Rhapsody on repeat. There's a lot of emotion packed into that one song." He lowered his gaze. "I wish I could feel any of it."

Oh boy. This was bad. I had to do something to help Father Kevin. "Have you considered seeking professional help? Or maybe even talking to another priest?"

"There's no point," he replied. "They don't see the world as clearly as I do now."

Okay, I certainly wasn't going to reason with him in his current state of mind. "If you think of anything that might have triggered this, will you call me?" I grabbed a pen and notepad from the bedside table closest to me and scribbled my number. "And if you feel like you need to talk to someone, my sister-in-law Verity is a doctor and an excellent listener." I added her number under mine.

"Thank you," he said, without glancing at me. "I've heard of Dr. Verity. People seem to like her a lot."

No surprise there. Verity was pretty great.

I stood to go. "I'll let you get back to your…lounging," I said.

He clicked the remote and resumed his program.

"Just out of curiosity, is that Real Housewives?" I asked.

"New York," he said. "It's the best of the franchises. They're genuinely friends. It isn't staged like The Hills. If the pearly gates existed, those MTV people certainly wouldn't be gaining admittance, I can say that with confidence."

"Good to know."

"I'm sorry I wasn't more help to you," Father Kevin said. "I know that's my role, or it was."

"I wasn't here for me, Father," I said. "I was here for you." He grunted, as though that was a strange thing for me to say, and turned back to the television.

Last Ark was a beautiful new boat that comfortably seated around twelve people. I briefly wondered whether dark magic was the reason they could afford a boat as nice as this one.

"Mr. Masterson?" I called. The boat seemed empty and quiet. It rocked gently, and the only sound was the water lapping against it. "Mrs. Masterson?"

I boarded the boat and hoped I didn't find them in an uncompromising position on the floor. Some things could not be unseen. Before I could move any further, I heard a noise behind me. I whirled around to see a middle-aged couple on the dock. The man was medium height and build with a gorgeous head of salt and pepper hair. Men managed to age so gracefully that it irked me sometimes. The woman's brown hair was streaked with gray and she wore a pair of tortoiseshell frames that made her round face look even rounder. Their arms were laden with grocery bags.

"Can I help you?" the man asked. He didn't look pleased to find a stranger on his boat.

I whipped out my badge. "Sorry to bother you. I'm Agent Eden Fury. Are you Paul and Judy Masterson?"

"We are," Paul said.

"I was hoping to ask you a few questions about Father Kevin."

Mrs. Masterson gasped. "He's not in trouble, is he? Please don't tell me it's anything to do with pornography."

Mr. Masterson silenced her with a look. "Why do you always overreact? You know perfectly well Father Kevin isn't into anything inappropriate." He climbed onto the boat and set the bags aside. "You'll have to excuse my wife. She has an overactive imagination."

Judy followed her husband's lead and set her bags on the floor of the boat. "How can we help you?"

"Father Kevin said he was with you on Friday," I said. "Did you notice anything strange about his behavior then?"

"Not at all," Paul said. "We had a pleasant day on the water. Father Kevin loves spending time on the boat with us."

"I packed sandwiches," Judy said. "We chatted about our trip to Vatican City. Different types of fish we tend to see in the bay versus the ocean."

"It was a normal day with him," Paul added.

"How long were you together?"

"If I had to guess, I'd say five hours." Paul looked to his wife for confirmation and she nodded. "We went out into the

Atlantic and then turned around and came back. It was nice but uneventful."

"He didn't mention anything about losing faith or feeling conflicted?" I asked.

"No, nothing like that," Paul said. "He talked about a couple of church fundraisers that Judy and I are helping him with. All very positive."

"Would you mind if I looked around your boat?" I asked. If Paul and Judy were secretly into dark magic, I'd be able to spot evidence.

"Is that necessary?" Paul asked.

"It'll only take a minute," I said.

"Do you have a warrant?" Paul asked.

Judy gave her husband's arm a firm smack. "You'll have to excuse my husband. He's been acting a little more paranoid than usual the past couple of days." She laughed anxiously. "Last night he accused me of deliberately leaving the lid off the toothpaste to annoy him."

"Because you did," Paul practically snarled. "And you left the pantry door open again too. You know I can't stand that. Why are you trying to get under my skin?"

Judy tossed me a pointed look.

"Paul, would you mind checking the galley to see if Father Kevin left anything behind?" I asked. "A packet of tissues. Anything really."

"Sure."

Once he disappeared, I turned to Judy, keeping my voice low. "I take it this behavior isn't typical of your husband."

"No, Paul is always so level-headed and reasonable," Judy said quietly. "It's one of his most attractive qualities. I thought maybe it was because he'd started smoking again and then tried to quit before I caught him."

"Did you ask him about it?"

"He denied it and then accused me of snooping on him."

She shook her head. "I had to laugh it off. What else could I do?"

Hmm. Could they have tried to perform a spell that backfired on Paul and impacted Father Kevin? I didn't sense any residual magic, only the normal amount of energy. Chipping Cheddar had more than its share thanks to the vortex and the portal, but *Last Ark* didn't seem to make my fury senses tingle.

Paul stomped around the galley for good measure and returned empty-handed. "Nothing."

"Thanks for checking," I said. "Tell me, did you all eat the same food the day Father Kevin visited?"

Judy's brow wrinkled. "I think so. I packed lunches and we all had water."

"I had a beer," Paul said.

"Or two," Judy said, using a slightly chastising tone.

"Did Father Kevin?" I asked.

Judy shook her head. "No. He doesn't drink."

It didn't sound like they were influenced by anything they digested. "Did Father Kevin mention anything else he'd done that day, either before he arrived or afterward?"

Judy snapped her fingers. "He'd had a coffee at Magic Beans with someone from church before he came here." She knocked Paul's elbow. "Who was it again, Paul? That pretty blonde with the brilliant smile."

"Sassy," Paul said.

I nearly choked. "Sassy Persimmons?"

"That's right. She always comes alone."

"And wears yoga gear," Judy said, wrinkling her nose in disapproval. "Sometimes I miss the formality of the old days."

I didn't even realize that Sassy was Catholic. "Thanks, that's helpful." I glanced helplessly around the boat. It seemed like *Last Ark* was a dead end.

"Will there be anything else?" Paul asked, somewhat impatiently.

"Let her look, Paul," Judy said. "You're being uncooperative. It makes you look like you have something to hide."

"I'm not even sure what you're looking for," Paul said. "Do you think we made Father Kevin want to leave the church? Like we blackmailed him or something?"

"And I'm the one who overreacts," Judy remarked wryly. "Why don't you check the galley yourself, Agent Fury?"

A quick sweep of the area showed me that Paul and Judy were nothing more than a typical suburban middle-aged couple with a nice boat. They didn't even have a single candle on board. No evidence of blood or antiques. Nothing.

"Thank you so much for your time," I said, returning to them. "I really appreciate it. Sorry for the intrusion."

"We hope Father Kevin changes his mind soon," Judy said. "Church won't be the same without him."

"I'm sure many of the parishioners feel the same," I said. "Have a good day."

I left the boat and walked along the dock, thinking about our conversation. Father Kevin and Paul Masterson had both started acting out of character around the same time. That couldn't be a coincidence. The question was—why?

CHAPTER SEVEN

I SAT at the table in the kitchen, contemplating the checkerboard. Something seemed wrong, but I couldn't put my finger on it.

"Are you going to move, Eden?" Aunt Thora asked. "It's almost past my bedtime." She took a dainty sip of her tea.

"I had a move worked out, but I must've made a mistake," I said. It wasn't often that I played checkers. Olivia and I had enjoyed a pretend game recently where she'd spent most of the time stacking the pieces on top of each other and letting Ryan knock them over.

"You didn't make a mistake," Aunt Thora said. "I cheated when you got up to get a glass of water. I moved that piece over so that I can jump you on my next turn." She tapped one of the red checkers.

Grandma glanced up from the sofa where she was playing Little Critters. "You've gone soft in your old age, Thora."

"You're calling her soft because she admitted to cheating?" I asked. "In my book, that's called honesty and integrity."

"Your book is boring," Grandma said, and returned her focus to the phone. "I'm stealing this boy's critter from his zoo and replacing it with the pink sparkly one. He'll have a meltdown when he sees it tomorrow."

I shook my head. "Why would you cheat at checkers?" And then immediately admit to it?

Aunt Thora shrugged. "Old habits die hard, I guess. I used to do a lot worse."

"See?" Grandma said. "Soft."

The sound of the front door alerted us to my mother's arrival. Inwardly I groaned. I'd hoped to be safely in the attic before she came home from her date so that I could be spared the salacious details.

"This was the worst date ever," my mother proclaimed. She sashayed past us in her pale pink backless dress. Diamonds glittered on her lobes and wrist.

"Did he try to pay you at the end?" Grandma asked.

My mother glared at her.

"Tell us what happened, Beatrice," Aunt Thora said encouragingly.

"It's what didn't happen," my mother said. She tossed her purse onto the coffee table and it skidded across to rest on the edge.

Personally, I was relieved that something didn't happen, whatever that something was.

"Care to elaborate?" Grandma asked.

"I simply can't talk about it." My mother flopped dramatically on the sofa in a way that suggested we would not be able to leave this space without talking about it.

"I vote for waterboarding," Grandma said. "That'll speed things up."

"Shall I make tea?" Aunt Thora asked. "Or hot water with lemon?"

"And honey," my mother added. "And a teensy bit of gin." She held her finger and thumb an inch apart.

Aunt Thora dutifully headed to the stovetop to heat the kettle.

"What happened?" Grandma pressed. I noticed that she kept her eyes locked on the screen.

"I had my date with Fernando tonight, that lovely man from the bakery." She leaned against the back of the sofa and closed her eyes. "He's absolutely dreamy. His legs are like walking around on two oak trees. You can only imagine what's between them."

"A twig and berries?" Grandma suggested.

"Hardly." My mother cleared her throat, trying to pull herself together. "We went back to his place. Such a tidy little house. I was very impressed. He had these sweet curtains over the window in the kitchen..."

Aunt Thora delivered a steaming mug to the end table. "I don't think anyone's interested in the curtains, dear."

"No, I guess not." My mother sat up and opened her eyes. "Well, the long and the short of it is that I couldn't enjoy either the long or the short of it. Believe me, I tried every which way."

I cringed. "Am I necessary for this conversation?"

"If I have to suffer, then so do you," Grandma said. "What was the problem? Too much alcohol with dinner?"

"The problem wasn't him." My mother shuddered. "The problem was me." She lifted the mug to her lips and took a careful sip. "That never, ever happens. I mean never." She looked at me. "You can ask your father."

I pressed my lips together. "I'd rather not, thanks."

"Fernando is gorgeous." My mother grew dewy-eyed just talking about him. "Such a powerful body. And those hands are made for kneading dough. Just think about what they're capable of on a woman's body."

"Okay, we get it," Grandma said. "What are we supposed to do about it?"

"I don't know what's wrong with me," my mother said. "What if this is the end?"

"You're not going to die without sex," I said. I knew that for a fact.

"I might," she shot back. "This might signal the end of my fertility."

"You passed fertility about a decade ago," Grandma said. "Your sex drive is another story. That shouldn't be giving you any grief. It's not like you're out of practice."

"Certainly not," my mother said. "Anyway, I was so embarrassed that I left Fernando in a hurry. I even left my underpants behind."

"I'm surprised you bothered to wear any in the first place," Grandma said.

"I bought a new matching set on Saturday. Aunt Thora was with me."

I scrunched my nose. "You went shopping with her for sex clothes?"

"I didn't mean to," Aunt Thora admitted. "We went into town for the market and ended up passing one of the bars with the nice outdoor patio."

"What does that have to do with anything?" I asked.

"It was teeming with older gentlemen," Aunt Thora said.

"Exactly," my mother chimed in. "It reminded me that I needed new underpants for my date, so we went to that wonderful boutique off Pimento Plaza."

"I bought a bra that no one will see," Aunt Thora said. "It's pretty though. You can bury me in that one. Makes my boobs look good when I'm lying down."

My mother stared absently into her mug. "I don't know what I'll do if I can't enjoy sex anymore." She glanced at Aunt Thora. "What would you do if you couldn't enjoy lemons anymore?"

My great-aunt contemplated the question. "Grow peaches

instead? I mean, it wouldn't be the same, but I guess I could try."

"There's your answer, Beatrice," Grandma said. "You can become a lesbian."

"You don't just *become* a lesbian," I said.

"Speak to Moyer," Grandma said. "He'll advise you."

"Uncle Moyer is not a lesbian," I said tersely. "Nor is he their appointed representative."

"Well, who is?" my mother asked in earnest. "I should probably arrange a meeting now, just in case."

I swallowed a cry of frustration. "Mom, maybe you weren't as into Fernando as you think. Or maybe it was an off night. Everybody has an off night on occasion. Don't rush to judgment."

My mother played with her earring. "You're right. I should give him another try before I make any rash decisions." She whipped out her phone. "I'm going to text him right now and arrange to collect my underpants." She smiled as she began tapping the screen and nausea rolled over me. I didn't want to imagine my mother sexting Fernando, or anyone else for that matter.

"I thought of something else," Grandma said.

"For what?" my mother asked, still typing.

"My funeral," Grandma said.

My mother and I exchanged glances. "You really have suggestions?" my mother asked.

"I want to choose the music," Grandma said. "I'd like to start with *Rebel Yell* by Billy Idol and end with a real blood pumper like *Immigrant Song*."

I balked. "You want us to play Led Zeppelin at your funeral?"

Grandma waved a hand. "Sure. Why not?"

I drank more of my water, but not too much or I'd have

to get up for a refill. I didn't want Aunt Thora to take another opportunity to cheat.

"Whatever you do for my funeral, please don't talk about my fury traits," I said. "It's bad enough I have to live with them. I don't want them to be my defining characteristics in death too."

My mother focused on me. "You don't appreciate what you have. If it weren't for those fury traits of yours, you wouldn't be the agent you are. You're looking in that glass and seeing it half empty when everyone else sees it as half full."

"You think my achievements are the result of being a fury?" That was downright insulting. I'd worked hard to get to this point. Well, not *this* point. I'd worked hard to become an FBI agent. The FBM was basically the consolation prize.

"Your strength, your stamina, your immortality," my mother said. "You can even fly if you want to, although I know you think those wings are undignified."

"Invisible snakes now live on my head," I said. "If you think that somehow makes me better at my job, you don't really understand what I do."

Grandma got up from the sofa and wandered into the kitchen. "Let me tell you a little story." She retrieved a small shot glass from the cabinet and set it on the table next to mine. "Once upon a time there was a girl who viewed the world through black and white glasses." Grandma dumped the water from my glass into the shot glass. "There, your cup runneth over. Problem solved. Now stop complaining and go do whatever it is you actually do."

I stared at the full glass of water for a long beat. Finally I picked it up and drained the glass dry. "I'm going to bed, which is what I wanted to do over an hour ago." I slammed the empty glass back on the table and retreated to the attic without another word.

. . .

The next morning, I took Princess Buttercup on a walk through the neighborhood and then circled back to the house to check on John's progress with the barn. John Maclaren was a carpenter my parents had hired to renovate the barn on the border between their properties so that I had my own place to live. Watching work on the barn was like watching for the kettle to boil. John never seemed to be working fast enough. Granted, his work had been hampered by supernatural forces along the way, but still. I was starting to feel desperate for my own space. It wasn't lost on me that the sooner I moved into the barn, the sooner Chief Fox could visit me without fear of running into my mother on the attic steps.

"How's it going, John?" I asked, as I entered the shell of the barn.

The carpenter stood in the middle staring at the ceiling. "Not very well."

"What's the problem now?"

John dropped his gaze to me. "I feel like I've lost my vision of what this place can be."

"That's why you have plans," I said. "You can refer to them and remember."

"I don't know," he said, somewhat listless. "I'm not sure they speak to me anymore."

"Of course they don't speak to you. They're on paper," I said.

"But this is an art form," he argued. "It's not like one of those HGTV shows. This barn has history and deserves to have the right vision executed. I'm going to ruin it if I'm not careful."

"You're never going to finish it if you're not careful," I said.

John scratched his head. "I know I can shape this into something amazing. I just need to refocus. Maybe I should go back to meditation." He pulled out his phone. "There's an app I can use to get into the right headspace."

"I don't care what it takes," I said. My impatience was on full display now and I felt a little guilty about it. John was a nice guy.

"I haven't felt this lost since before I decided to become a carpenter," he said.

"What about when you won the lottery?" I asked. "You seemed pretty lost then, too."

"No, this is worse." He sat on a wooden beam that should have been affixed to the ceiling weeks ago. "I think I'll dip into my watercolors and see if that inspires me."

"Do what you have to do, John." I left the barn and whistled for Princess Buttercup before my temper got the better of me.

I let the hellhound into the house and snuck upstairs to change before anyone spotted me. Chief Fox and I had arranged to meet at the portal and I didn't want to be late. He was interested in seeing its location so that he could also monitor the area for strange activity. I knew Neville would freak out that I shared confidential information, but I decided it was in the town's best interest to have multiple sets of eyes watching for trouble. The chief patrolled the park most days, so it made sense to tell him the truth about 'the mound.'

"So this is the portal?" Chief Fox asked. He stood in front of the sealed entrance and examined it. "Doesn't look like a barrier between us and an entire supernatural world."

"I wouldn't recommend kicking it," I said. "Those rocks are pretty hard. You might break a toe."

"And we're here because a priest doesn't want to be a priest anymore?"

"It's not that simple," I said. "Father Kevin is acting out of character and so is Paul Masterson."

"And that means there might be demonic leakage from the portal?"

I scrunched my nose. "That sounds gross."

He chuckled. "It does, doesn't it?"

"I do a daily check on the portal regardless of what's going on and log the results for the FBM," I explained. "When there's a potential issue like this one, I'll take a closer look and make sure no energy's getting through."

"Has energy ever gotten through before?"

"No, but just because a portal has been dormant for centuries doesn't mean it will stay that way," I said. "It pays to be vigilant." Because the price for not being vigilant would be catastrophic.

"I don't think Paul Masterson is the only one who's paranoid," he teased.

I popped a hand on my hip. "Do you want to learn or not?"

"Teach me your ways, Master Jedi." He placed his palms together and bowed.

"Trust me, if this force busts open at the seams, you'll wish it was someone as adorable as Darth Vader."

His smile dissolved. "But you said guns don't work on your Otherworld folks, so what else could I do?"

"You'd report it to me," I said. "And then you'd get yourself somewhere safe. The FBM would take care of it."

"What about the vortex? Should I be able to feel the energy there if it's that powerful?"

"I don't think you would," I said. "You're not tuned to it. If you did feel something, you wouldn't recognize it for what it was. Humans aren't designed that way."

The chief surveyed the space. "I can't believe this place is basically hidden in plain sight of the whole town."

"It's not just the portal," I said. "All supernaturals are basically hidden in plain sight."

The chief sauntered around the interior of the mound, tapping on the rocky walls and pressing his ear to one of the larger boulders.

"What are you doing?" I asked.

"I just want to see if I can hear anything happening in Otherworld." He cupped his hands around his mouth. "Hello from the other side!"

I shook my head. "You're not going to burst into an Adele song, are you?"

He turned to face me, his expression serious. "If I did, would you dance with me?" Before I could react, his arm was around my waist and he pulled me taut against his body. His hand slid into mine. "How about it, Agent Fury? Do you dance?"

"I don't really get the chance." It felt strangely intimate to be in his arms in the privacy of the hillside. No one could see us. Most residents didn't know this place existed.

"You look deep in thought," the chief remarked. "I didn't expect my question to provoke such a look of consternation."

"Is that what I have right now?" I asked.

He touched the spot between my eyebrows. "Yep. Right there. Deep thinking happening."

I was acutely aware of the proximity of our bodies. Of his sea-colored eyes burning into mine. The intensity of his gaze told me exactly what he was thinking. I smiled. "Kissing is the same as dancing, right? The tongue tango?"

He grinned. "I wouldn't object to giving my tongue a little exercise. It gets tired of the same routine day in and day out."

I laughed and pulled away slightly. "What kind of routine is that?"

"Eating, of course. What did you think, pervert?"

Instead of kissing him, I rested my head on his shoulder and let him sway me in a slow circle. He started to hum the melody to *Fly Me to the Moon* by Frank Sinatra.

"If any demons are watching from the other side, I guess they'll think this is odd," he said. "That a human is dancing with a fury."

"They'll assume it's a mating ritual that ends with one of us getting our head bitten off."

"Sexy and dangerous, my favorite combination."

"That explains a lot." My hands slipped from around his neck to rest on his chest. "We should probably go."

He lifted one of my hands and kissed it. "How about we finish the song first? It's an oldie but goodie."

"As long as you don't need me to sing."

"Nope. Just rest your weary head here and I'll do the rest."

I snuggled against him, enjoying the way his chest vibrated as he hummed. As much as I hated to admit it, maybe Grandma was right. Maybe my cup runneth over after all.

CHAPTER EIGHT

By the time I arrived in the small room at the back of Chophouse, my cousin Rafael's restaurant, for the supernatural council meeting, I was still humming *Fly Me to the Moon.* Earlier, Neville had heard me humming it in the office and bombarded me with more Frank Sinatra facts than one wizard had any right to know.

Aggie Grace greeted me with a warm smile. As one of my neighbors on Munster Close, I'd known Aggie and her sisters my whole life but not in a professional capacity until my return to town. Once I'd assumed Paul Pidcock's role as the local FBM agent, I'd also assumed his position on the council. The members kept tabs on the supernatural community-at-large and discussed any pressing issues, like the fairies' petition to keep drones on the ground. Apparently, more than one fairy had collided in midair with a human's Christmas or birthday present and the fairies had banded together to request a ban.

"Evenin', Eden." Husbourne Crawley played with a toothpick in his mouth. He wore one of his signature pale linen suits. His complementary hat rested on the back of the chair. Although I knew he was a wizard, in my mind he would always be Foghorn Leghorn. Husbourne was another neighbor on Munster Close, and I'd spent years of adolescence picturing the rooster from the cartoons whenever I passed him on the street.

"Good to see you," I said, taking a seat next to him at the round table. "Your garden is thriving. That crape myrtle is gorgeous."

"Surprised you noticed," he drawled. "If I recall correctly, nature isn't really your thing."

My cheeks flamed. "Okay, maybe I didn't. Aunt Thora mentioned it when we went for a drive and I seconded her opinion."

"Never you mind," said Aggie. "It was sweet of you to pay him the compliment."

Adele LeRoux looked effortlessly chic in a beautiful silk headscarf and a crisp white blouse. The witch leaned forward to examine me. "Are you wearing earrings, Eden?"

My fingers brushed against the silver hoop. "My ears have been pierced since high school. I figured I should wear them more often so the holes don't close up." And maybe because Chief Fox mentioned in passing that he liked them.

Adele continued to observe me for an extended moment, as though she sensed the sudden appearance of earrings was significant. As my grandmother's witchy rival, Adele would love to know information about me that my own family didn't. Like Grandma, Adele was the powerful matriarch of her magical family, except her coven hailed from Louisiana and they were among the first black families in Chipping Cheddar.

"Shame about Corinne and Chief Fox," Adele said idly. "I thought they made a fine couple."

I swallowed hard. Had Corinne told her grandmother the reason she broke up with the chief? "These things happen," I said, noncommittal.

"They both seem to have taken it in stride," Aggie said, saving me without realizing it. "She's got a new business to run and he's still new to the town. They're both young. Makes sense to focus on their professional lives."

"How's Magic Beans faring after its little setback?" Husbourne asked. The shop had been closed soon after opening because of a demonic parasite.

"Wonderful," Adele said. "We couldn't be more pleased for her."

"A thriving business is good for the town too," Hugh Phelps said, swaggering into the room. The werewolf dropped into the seat next to Adele. "I haven't missed the appetizers, have I?" Hugh generally seemed more intent on the food than the meeting.

"Of course not, darling," Aggie said. "Rafael hasn't been back here yet."

"That's because this place is mobbed tonight," I said. Chophouse was one of the most successful restaurants in town and we were lucky to be able to meet here in private.

On cue, the door flew open to reveal Rafael, who greeted us with a dazzling smile. "Sorry to keep you waiting, esteemed members of the council. It's hectic out there tonight."

"No worries, son," Husbourne said. "We're not in a rush."

"Can I interest anyone in appetizers?" Rafael asked. "I'll make sure to expedite your order...without sacrificing quality, of course." The warlock took great pride in his work.

"The usual round of drinks, please," Adele said. "And the avocado yogurt dip with the pita chips."

Aggie brightened. "That sounds simply delicious."

"The crab and avocado toast for me," Husbourne said. "It melts in your mouth, ya'll. You have to try it."

"You're so incredibly talented, Rafael," Aggie said.

Rafael bowed, the hint of a smile on his lips. "I aim to please the palette."

Adele smiled. "You're a true genius."

Hugh wiggled a hand in the air. "I'd like the truffle ravioli, but can I get it with cheddar cheese instead of Calcagno?"

Rafael sucked in a breath. "I beg your pardon?"

Uh oh.

"I like cheddar," Hugh said. "Don't grate it too fine either. I prefer it chunky so I can taste it."

"Calcagno is a type of pecorino," Rafael said. "The sweetness and aroma are perfect for the truffle..."

"Yeah, see. I'm not a big fan of Pecorino," Hugh said.

Rafael's face turned bright red. "As I'm sure you can appreciate, I'm well-versed in which cheese is better suited to the dishes I create."

"And as I'm sure you can appreciate," Hugh said, "I grew up in a town that worships cheese, so I know my pecorino from my cheddar."

Rafael struggled to maintain control. "As you wish, Mr. Phelps," he ground out.

"Thanks, buddy," Hugh said, with a smug grin.

"Locking the door behind me as usual," Rafael said. "Eden, Julie asked me to tell you that she and Meg will be dining here within the hour and to please find them on your way out."

"Absolutely," I said.

Aggie waved a bony hand. "I propose we get started. I suffered a terrible bout of insomnia last night and I intend to be out like a light before the clock strikes ten."

"You poor thing," Adele said. "It's the age. I know how that feels."

Aggie proceeded to read the minutes from the last meeting.

"Any news from the town council?" Hugh asked.

"We had our meeting yesterday, in fact," Husbourne said. It was tradition to have one member sit on both the supernatural and human council as a way of streamlining information and cutting down on gossip. Of course, the human town council didn't know that Husbourne was essentially a double agent.

"Uneventful?" Adele asked.

"Not entirely," Husbourne said. "Mayor Whitehead requested a dedicated parking spot."

"That doesn't seem unreasonable," Adele said. "Spots can be hard to come by, especially during festivals or tourist season."

Husbourne hesitated. "She requested a dedicated parking spot at the waterfront."

The waterfront was prime real estate. The town earned revenue from the parking meters near the promenade.

"That doesn't sound like Wilhelmina," Aggie said. "Are you sure you understood her correctly?"

"Oh, quite sure," Husbourne said. "The council said we'd discuss it and take a vote. We all seemed to be having the same thought."

"Maybe she's ill," Hugh suggested. "She knows it will hamper her ability to walk, but she's not ready to share the news yet."

"Unlikely," Adele said.

"But not impossible," Hugh shot back.

Aggie made a contemplative sound. "Well, I guess we'll have to wait and see how that plays out. Keep us updated, Husbourne."

Rafael pushed open the door with his back and swung into the room with our drinks and appetizers. He set the tray on a side table and distributed the small glasses of sweet-smelling golden liquid first. Fairy Dust was an old recipe that Aggie had given to Rafael so that the council could enjoy the closest drink to nectar that existed in this world.

I tipped back my glass and let the liquid coat my tongue and throat. It tasted every bit as amazing as it smelled.

"I could devour this whole," Adele said, eyeing the plate of avocado yogurt dip and chips. It was arranged in the design of a flower. "Rafael, you are such an artist."

Hugh admired the chunks of cheddar cheese that covered his ravioli. "Looks good." He shoveled a forkful into his mouth and chewed.

Rafael's smile tightened. "Normally one does not simply *break clumps* of *cheddar* on truffle ravioli—the Calcagno is finely grated so as to..."

Hugh held up a hand. "This is better than the Trio Burger over at the diner. I think I've helped you create a new winner, Rafael. You can thank me later."

The warlock wisely fled the room before he said something he'd regret.

Aggie continued with the meeting, clearly desperate to get home and climb into bed. "We need to talk about Mrs. Huntington."

"Do we have to?" Hugh complained.

"She claims she saw werewolves near her flowerbeds again," Aggie said.

Everyone groaned.

"That gnome needs to be banned from filing complaints," Husbourne said, exasperated.

"Hugh, is there any chance she's right this time?" Adele asked.

Hugh shrugged. "Doubtful. Nobody in the pack likes to go near her cats. They're small but feisty."

"Do we think she's fed up enough to call the police station this time?" Aggie said. "We don't want her spouting off to Chief Fox about werewolves. He'll want her to see a psychiatrist."

"I'll talk to her this time," I offered. It wasn't fair to make Adele do it every time.

Hugh tapped his fork rhythmically on the edge of the table. "What if she does call the cops?"

"Then I'll talk to Chief Fox too," I said. And if I was lucky, we'd do more than talk. Merciful gods. I had to stop thinking like that in front of others. I was sure they could figure out everything from the expression on my face.

"He seems sharp," Hugh said. "I almost wonder if it's going to be a problem. Chief O'Neill was a good guy, but not the brightest bulb on the Christmas tree."

"The chief won't be a problem," I said, almost too quickly.

"You know him best," Adele said. "We trust your judgment."

"Any FBM news, Eden?" Husbourne asked.

"As you know, the pod demons were taken care of," I said. "Daily checks of the portal show that it's still dormant."

Adele threw a pinch of salt over her shoulder for luck.

"I did have an incident with a vampire recently," I said. "She was stalking people at The Cheese Wheel. Her name was Gloria and she said she was from out of town and visiting a friend."

"Did she touch anyone?" Hugh asked, snarling. Werewolves and vampires weren't exactly the best of friends, even though they lived in the same small town.

"No, I made sure of it," I said, "but she seemed almost upset by her own behavior. It was strange."

"Speaking of strange behavior," Aggie said, "is everyone aware of Father Kevin's decision to leave the church?"

"I spoke to him about it," I said. "Ted O'Neill was really upset, so Aunt Thora asked me to talk to the priest and see if there was anything magical at work."

"People lose faith every day," Hugh said dismissively. "Why would she worry that magic was behind it?"

"She and Ted are very close," Aggie interjected. "I'm sure she's worried about her friend's state of mind. It hasn't been very long since Ted lost his brother, remember."

"While we're on the subject of losing folks, is anyone else attending Myrtle's funeral later this week?" Adele asked.

"My family is," I said. "Well, not my dad, but my mom, Grandma, and Aunt Thora."

Adele's lips stretched into a polite smile. "I look forward to seeing them."

"You don't have to lie," I said. "I don't look forward to seeing them and I have to do it every day." Okay, that was probably a little harsh with regard to Aunt Thora. She was a gem.

"I think it's lovely the way the witches have banded together to host her funeral," Aggie said.

"We're not all bad," Adele said, with a pointed look at me. I didn't need Adele to educate me on my family. I was an expert.

We finished the remainder of our drinks and appetizers and I noted that not a morsel of food was left on anyone's plate. Rafael would be pleased.

"See ya'll later," Husbourne said. He stood and stretched before retrieving his hat from the back of the chair.

"I'm off to bed," Aggie said. "Hope tonight is better for me."

"Eden, would you mind staying put?" Adele asked. "I'd like a quick word."

"Sure." My stomach twisted into a giant pretzel. If Adele asked me about my relationship with Chief Fox, I would have to lie straight to her face. The thought made me queasy.

"Let us know what happens with Mrs. Huntington," Hugh said.

Once everyone vacated the room, Adele clasped her hands on the table. "I'd like to talk to you about Rosalie."

I would have jumped for joy if I hadn't been seated. "What about her?"

"I hadn't thought to mention it until the meeting," Adele began. "Father Kevin is making me wonder…" She tapped her French tips on the table. "Rosalie has been acting oddly."

What else was new? Rosalie LeRoux was by far the worst of the LeRoux witches. She was more interested in money and men than magic and had no problem pretending to have skills that she didn't. If you needed a fake psychic for your bridal shower, Rosalie was your witch.

"How so?" I asked.

Adele appeared thoughtful for a moment. "Disconnected from reality, as though she isn't sure what's real and what isn't."

"A psychotic break?" I asked. That could be very serious for a witch with Rosalie's abilities.

"No, I don't think so." Adele played with the hem of her headscarf. "It's more…" She shook her head. "Never mind. I'm sure I'm making connections where none exist. I'm just worried about my daughter. She's always been someone I have to keep an eye on, you see."

"I understand," I said.

"Forget I mentioned it, won't you?"

"Forget what?" I said, and smiled.

"You're good people, Eden, in spite of your upbringing."

"Thanks. That means a lot." I followed Adele out of the private room and scanned the main dining area for Rafael's wife and sixteen-year-old daughter. I caught sight of them at their usual table in the far corner. They were in the midst of a heated conversation when I approached.

"But I didn't get in touch to tell you I'd be late," Meg said. "Why didn't you send out a search party or a helicopter? Don't you love me anymore?"

"You're a big girl," Julie said. "I knew you were fine."

"You didn't even text my friends," Meg said, visibly annoyed. "What's the point of keeping all their numbers in your phone if you're not prepared to use them?"

"I've deleted them," Julie said.

I pulled up a chair. "Is this some kind of reverse psychology experiment?" Julie was notoriously anxious about her daughter's well-being. Every nightmare scenario seemed to end with Meg dead in a ditch.

Meg pointed a finger at her mother. "See? That's what I said too."

Julie held up her hands in acquiescence. "It's not, I swear. I'm just confident that your father and I have taught you well and that you'll be okay out n the world on your own."

Meg and I exchanged glances. Definitely reverse psychology.

"How was your meeting?" Julie asked. "I'm so glad you've come back to Chipping Cheddar. I know the town is safe in your capable hands."

Meg's eyes bulged. "Aren't you the same werewolf who thought that Dad should put some magical wiretap in the police station so we could be updated on any crimes in progress and avoid the area?"

I didn't dare mention that Neville had done exactly that. I'd have to make sure I didn't slip and mention it to the chief now that he knew about the work Neville and I did.

"I've been seeing things more clearly," Julie said. "I think it's terrific that you don't want a phone or any of the technological trappings of your generation. You'll be better for it."

Meg's jaw unhinged. "You're not going to try and open a secret Instagram account in my name so I look normal?" She put air quotes around the word 'normal.'

"What about sneaking photos of her and pretending she took a selfie," I added.

Julie held up a hand as though she were swearing an oath. "No, I promise I will never do that again."

Meg's brow lifted. "Mark this day on your calendars, folks."

"Your paper calendar and my phone because I am completely cool with you only writing down appointments the old-fashioned way," Julie said.

"I'm a witness," I said.

"How's the single life, Eden?" Julie asked. "Your mother said you spend most of your free time in the attic watching television."

"Oh, did she?"

Meg suppressed a smile.

"My *life* is fine," I said. "It's plenty busy without a husband and children."

"The right guy will come along when you least expect it," Julie said. "That's how it was for me. I never dreamed I'd marry a warlock of all supernaturals."

"Thanks, but I'm content with the way things are," I said. Content to spend secret sexy time with Sawyer Fox dancing to Frank Sinatra.

"I want to be like you when I grow up, Eden." Meg looked at me with stars in her eyes.

"What are you talking about? You're more grown up at sixteen than I am now," I said.

"You're so sure of yourself," Meg said. "And you live life on your own terms, no matter how much pressure you get from your family."

I smiled at her. "You seem to be doing a pretty good job of

that yourself, Miss Hipster."

"Mom still treats me like I'm six," Meg sulked.

"I do not." Julie threaded her fingers together. "Now, would you like chocolate or vanilla ice cream with sprinkles for dessert?"

CHAPTER NINE

"THIS PLACE IS GOING to be so cool when it's finished," Sassy said. She sat on a yoga mat on the floor of the barn. John had decided to meditate on his boat today and hope for inspiration to strike, so I knew the barn was a safe place to meet Sassy and ask about Father Kevin.

"Not when," I said. "If. John is great, but he seems to get easily distracted."

Sassy curled into child's pose. "Well, I'm so pleased that you decided to seek help for your issue."

"I don't have an issue."

She turned and gave me a pointed look. "You're wound tighter than a yo-yo. That's not normal for someone our age and definitely not normal for someone as fit as you."

"You think I'm fit?"

Sassy rolled her eyes. "Eden, you're a federal agent. Yes, you're in decent shape."

"Thanks." I forgot about the criticism from five seconds ago and focused on the compliment.

"Let's see if we can get you more limber," Sassy said. "The chief will thank me for it."

"Hey," I said. "You can't talk about that."

"Relax, there's no one here," Sassy said. She tightened her ponytail. "And I can keep a secret, though I don't get why you wouldn't want to slap a 'taken' sign on that broad chest. If women think he's available, you'll have your work cut out for you. Trust me, I know about dating a hot guy."

"I think I have some former experience to draw from," I reminded her.

Sassy flicked her fingers in a dismissive gesture. "That was high school. It doesn't really count." She pulled herself into a cross-legged position. "Let's start with basic breathing techniques."

I copied her pose and was immediately struck by how uncomfortable I was. "I can't sit in this position for too long. It bothers my back."

"It shouldn't," Sassy said. "You're probably out of alignment. Let me try to crack your back."

I recoiled. "What?" I imagined Sassy breaking my spine so that I spent the rest of my life being pushed around in a wheelchair by my mother. "Do not put your hands on my back!" I practically shrieked.

Sassy stared at me. "I can't understand what traumatic childhood events shaped you into…this." She waved a hand. "You seriously need to relax. Do I need to pour tequila down your throat before we stretch? Tell me what it takes."

I couldn't possibly explain to her what my childhood had really been like. The constant stress of wondering whether the pot your mother boiled on the stove contained someone's heart or whether your grandmother's muttering was an ancient curse about to be unleashed on an unsuspecting victim.

"You wouldn't understand," I said.

"Look, we all have invisible scars, right?" Sassy grabbed

my left leg and repositioned it slightly. "That's just part of the human existence. Yoga is the kind of activity that can help ease the pain."

"Is that why you go to church?" I asked.

She snapped back into position as though I'd struck her. "How do you know about that?"

"Someone mentioned it recently," I said. "They also said you were with Father Kevin at Magic Beans on Friday morning."

Sassy pursed her lips. "Is there something wrong with meeting a priest for coffee?"

I shrugged. "Depends on the reason, I guess."

"It's not like it was a date." She plucked an invisible thread on her yoga mat. "He's a good listener. I like talking to him."

"I didn't even realize you were Catholic."

She refused to meet my steady gaze. "I'm not."

"You're not Catholic, but you've been attending Sunday mass?"

"I go to confession too. Well, not anymore. Not with Father Kevin leaving." Sassy frowned. "It's a real bummer. It's hard to build that kind of trust with someone, especially a man."

"Does Father Kevin know you're not Catholic?"

She smiled. "I guess we both have our secrets."

Multiple questions rattled around in my brain, but I plucked the most obvious one from the bunch. "Why would you lie about being Catholic?"

Sassy placed her palms flat against each other and inhaled deeply. Once she released the breath, she said, "Because I overheard two ladies in the grocery store one day talking about how much they liked Father Kevin. That they felt uplifted every Sunday and it carried them through the week. I decided that I wanted to feel that way too." She snapped her fingers at me. "Do some breathing. Your shoulders look like they're ready to pull you into the air."

I put my hands together and drew a deep breath.

"Not like that," she scolded. "You sound like you're trapped in a box at the bottom of the ocean. Take your time and focus."

I made another attempt, making sure to slow my breathing.

"Better," she said. "Now do it again."

I'd forgotten how bossy Sassy could be. The head cheerleader was strong in this one. I took another breath and felt more relaxed this time.

"Why did you go to confession?" I asked. Did Sassy have sordid secrets to get off her chest?

She played with the tip of her ponytail. "It's sort of freeing to talk openly to someone who's duty-bound not to share. I mean, he has to answer to God if he mouths off. That's a real incentive to keep it under wraps."

"Did you tell him how you 'helped' Tanner cheat on me?"

She narrowed her eyes. "It's ancient history, Eden. I thought you'd moved past it."

I wiggled my butt to get more comfortable. "I'm not holding a torch, that's for sure."

"Good, you shouldn't. It's unhealthy to cling to negative emotions."

"A therapist would have the same duty, you know," I said.

"Yes, but a priest doesn't cost me anything," she said. "My insurance doesn't cover mental health services."

"What's been your impression of Father Kevin, up until he announced his departure?"

Sassy uncrossed her legs and stretched them straight out in front of her. "He's been wonderful. I've so looked forward to Sunday mornings. Listening to his powerful messages about redemption and loving thy neighbor. So overwhelmingly positive."

"Has Tanner ever gone with you?"

She snorted. "No way. He doesn't even know about it."

"Where does he think you go?"

"Yoga," she said. "Which I do, but not until afterward."

For someone with such uplifting messages, Father Kevin really seemed to have experienced an abrupt shift in outlook.

"Were you surprised by Father Kevin's announcement?" I asked.

"Of course. Who wasn't? It seemed to come completely out of the blue."

"He didn't mention anything at Magic Beans either?" I asked.

"Definitely not," she said. "He was his usual upbeat self. Gave me good advice and a positive quote to think about." She made a noise at the back of her throat. "Two are better than one…for if they fall, one will lift up the other." She flashed a proud smile. "That's from Ecclesiastes."

"He sounds like a wise man."

"Loosen your knees and bend forward at the waist," Sassy ordered.

I tried to do as instructed, but my muscles refused to cooperate.

"Why do you care if Father Kevin lost his faith?" she asked. "It's not like *you're* Catholic."

"I'm just interested. It's interesting."

Sassy studied me. "Okaaaay."

"What did you and Father Kevin talk about at Magic Beans?" I asked.

She hesitated. "What do you think?"

"Tanner?"

She nodded. "He's been a willing ear for me. Kind of like…" She trailed off.

"Like what?" I prodded.

She shifted to her hands and knees. "Like having a really good dad."

"I'm sorry," I said.

"You don't need to be sorry. Father Kevin's been a great father figure. Always full of good advice and never judged me."

"No, he saves all the judgment for his boss," I said.

Sassy made a face. "I told him how I was starting to second-guess my relationship with Tanner. That maybe I didn't really want to marry him after all."

"And what did Father Kevin say?"

"To follow the path that was calling to me, but not to give up on love."

"A flowery way of saying trust your gut."

"Pretty much." She offered a rueful smile. "I want kids. I want a messy house with signs of a chaotic but happy life. I want to step on Legos in the dark."

"You really don't," I said. "Olivia has left them on the floor at my mom's house and they hurt like you wouldn't believe." I copied her next pose and felt a twinge in my lower back. "You don't think you can have that life with Tanner?"

"I didn't have that life growing up and neither did he," she said. "I'm not sure that we'd be able to create something together that neither one of us has experience with. No role models."

I sensed there was more to it than that. "Do you worry that Tanner would leave once you have kids in the mix?"

She switched to her knees. "Not necessarily that he'd leave *because of* children—just that he would leave someday and we'd repeat the cycle."

"Do you love him?"

"I do, but I'm starting to wonder if I love him enough. If

we love each other enough. If we did, I think we'd be engaged by now."

"Do you worry that he'll cheat?" I asked. What possessed me to have this conversation with Sassy Persimmons of all people, I'd never know. High School Me was giving Adult Me a healthy dose of side eye.

Sassy pressed her forehead against the mat. "I worry about that all the time, given how we started." She rolled onto her side. "He travels for work so often. He meets sexy nurses all the time."

"They're not Halloween costumes," I said. "These are actual nurses."

"I know." Sassy returned to a seated position. "But if he did it to you, why not to me?"

"You just said it was ancient history." Not to mention ironic. It took two to cheat. Sassy hadn't cheated on anyone, but she'd certainly been a willing participant.

"I guess the bottom line is that I don't trust him and I'm not sure I ever will," Sassy said. "Is that someone I want to build a life with? Have children with?"

The answer to that question seemed pretty clear to me. I knew I'd dodged a bullet with Tanner, though the pain had been pretty fierce at the time.

"You're the only one who can answer that, Sassy."

"That's what Father Kevin said." She blew a strand of hair out of her eye. "Man, I'm really going to miss that guy."

I parked on the street in front of Mrs. Huntington's ranch-style house and walked along the brick path that delivered me to the front door via a small garden. The gnome clearly spent a lot of time cultivating her outdoor space. Everywhere I looked, flowers were blooming and plants were thriving.

The front door was open, leaving only a screen door

between us. Before I could call her name, two cats came charging at the door, meowing loudly.

"What is it, Hermione?" Mrs. Huntington appeared in the living room wearing a fuzzy pink bathrobe. She was short and sturdy with a mop of gray hair. "Ron, stop begging for food." She smiled when she spotted me. "Oh, hello. I didn't realize I had company."

"Hello, Mrs. Huntington," I said. "I'm Agent Eden Fury. I'm here on behalf of the supernatural council."

She peered at me through the screen. "They sent an agent? Is it that serious?" A third cat trotted over to investigate the scene and began weaving through the gnome's legs. "Stop that, Harry."

"I work for the Federal Bureau of Magic," I said. "I serve on the council as a volunteer. I offered to handle your garden issue." I glanced over my shoulder. "To be fair, though, your gardens are amazing. I know plenty of keen gardeners, but yours are truly impressive."

I thought the compliment might win her over. Instead, I seemed to agitate her.

"Not the side garden," she snapped. "I don't suppose you had a look there."

"No, ma'am. I didn't want to trespass."

The gnome opened the door and shooed the cats back into the house. "You three stay put. I'm not fast enough to catch you when you decide to do a runner." She hobbled down the steps and brushed past me. "Come on then, I'll show you."

We rounded the corner and she stopped in her tracks. It only took a moment to spot the problem—a patch of anemic flowers that looked like they'd been deprived of water and sunlight.

Mrs. Huntington jabbed a finger at the offending area.

"See what I mean? Werewolf piss is the only thing that will do that to my garden."

I highly doubted that. "Are you sure your cats haven't been sneaking outside?"

The gnome drew back, plainly offended by the accusation. "My cats are perfect angels. They would never be so vindictive as to ruin my garden. They know how important it is to me." She'd clearly never met Candy. My grandmother's cat would pee in the bathtub if you looked at her the wrong way.

"Have you actually seen any werewolves in the vicinity?" I asked. Her lot was somewhat off the beaten track but not completely isolated.

"I heard one howling the other night," she said. "My bedroom window was open and it sounded very close to the house. The cats went nuts so I shut the window and got out their thunder jackets."

"Thunder jackets?"

"The ones they wear during a thunderstorm to keep them from feeling anxious," the gnome explained. "Hermione is always trying to bite hers off, but the other two wear them quite happily."

"Are you sure it wasn't an owl or some other creature?"

She cemented her hands to her hips. "Do I seem deaf to you? I know the difference between a hoot and a howl."

"Of course you do. I didn't mean to imply otherwise." As much as I hated to do it, I crouched beside the dead flowers and sniffed. There was an acrid smell that could definitely be attributable to werewolves.

"See? It's werewolf, isn't it?" She almost sounded pleased.

"I'm not one hundred percent sure, but I haven't ruled it out." I resumed a standing position. "Was it only the one night that you heard the howling?"

"No, two nights in a row," she said. "I looked outside from

the upstairs window, but I couldn't see anything. I didn't want to actually go outside."

"Why do you think they'd be drawn to your garden?" I asked.

"They probably like the sweet scent of these flowers," she said. "I opened the window and yelled the other night, trying to scare them off, but I have no idea whether it worked because I couldn't see anything."

"I'm sorry you're dealing with this," I said. "If it's any consolation, no one can see this part of your garden unless they're standing right in front of it."

"I can see it," she said firmly. "I don't give a toss about what anybody else can see. I work hard on my garden. I don't want some interloper to destroy my handiwork."

"Totally understandable."

She crossed her arms. "And what are you going to do about it, Agent?"

"I'm going to do a little digging in the werewolf community and see what I can find out."

Her expression became skeptical. "You really believe me?"

"I believe that you heard howling and that a werewolf may have trespassed on your property," I said. "And I'll do my best to figure it out." I paused. "If it turns out a werewolf is responsible, what do you intend to do about it?"

"Make them pay compensation for my garden," she said. "I need to buy new flowers and replant them."

Well, that seemed reasonable. "You won't call the police, will you? Because that would make the issue more difficult to deal with."

Mrs. Huntington licked her lips, debating. "As much as I'd like a moment or two alone with that ruggedly handsome chief, I see your point."

Same, girl. Same. "I promise to get back to you as soon as I know anything."

The gnome looked me up and down. "Fury, did you say?"

"That's right."

"Beatrice and Stanley's daughter?"

Oh boy. "Yes, that's me."

"My husband used to have a crush on your mother," she said. "After she and Stanley divorced, he suggested we invite her over for cards to cheer her up." She tossed her head back and laughed. "What a moron. I mean, I miss him now that he's dead, but seriously." She shook her head. "Did he think I was stupid?"

I wasn't sure what to do with that information. I wanted to tell her that my mother would never stoop to dating a gnome, but that seemed like the wrong way to handle it.

"Men can be obtuse sometimes," I said vaguely.

"Well, you're much prettier than your mother."

I straightened. "Really? You think so?" No one ever said that. My mother was always being praised for her youthful beauty.

"Definitely. And you don't have that look that says you're going to hump any man that crosses your path."

"Um, thanks."

She continued to scrutinize me. "Your cousin is married to that werewolf, isn't he?" She harrumphed. "And you serve on the council with that Phelps fellow."

"Both are correct, but I have no qualms about putting a werewolf in his or her place for committing a misdemeanor. My job is to protect members of this community and that includes your garden from…werewolf pee."

"Glad to hear it." She finally seemed satisfied. "Would you like to come in for a glass of sweet tea? I'm sure the cats won't bite you." She hesitated. "Well, Hermione might, but she'll lick you first."

"As tempting as that offer is, I need to get going. There's a family dinner tonight and I have to change before my mother sees me."

She gave me a sympathetic nod. "Been there." She gestured to my head. "Maybe run a brush through that tangled mess, too. It looks like they got caught on tree branches on the way here."

Inwardly I sighed. Apparently everyone was a critic when it came to my appearance, even a gnome in a powder pink bathrobe.

CHAPTER TEN

I MANAGED to sneak up to the attic and change before anyone spotted me. I brushed my hair as per Mrs. Huntington's suggestion and even checked my teeth in the mirror.

"Why not wear a dress?" Alice asked, materializing. "You have such nice legs. You may as well show them off."

"Show them off to whom?" I asked. "It's a family dinner."

"Perhaps Chief Fox might happen by later," she said slyly.

I aimed the hairbrush at her. "You don't know anything, Alice."

She smiled demurely. "What's the problem, dear? It's not as though I can tell anyone."

I studied the ghost. "How do you know?"

"It's obvious when you're together that there's something between you. You're like two planets colliding."

"When did you see us together?" I didn't bother to hide the note of suspicion in my voice.

Alice turned to look behind her, as though someone had called her name. "What's that? Yes, I'll be right there!"

"Nice try," I said. "Have you been following me around town?"

Alice's ghostly form sank onto my mattress. "I've been trying to find more ways to amuse myself. There's only so much television I can watch before my head hurts."

"Same," I said. "You can visit other ghosts. Complain about the state of the world together and how terrible fashion is these days."

"I do on occasion." Her expression grew dreamy. "I thought it would be nice to pretend to be alive again, so I decided to follow you and see how you spent a typical day." She paused. "That reminds me—you really should stick to one donut, dear."

Heat warmed my cheeks. "Please don't cloak and dagger me. It's unsettling."

A smile played upon her lips. "He is so very handsome. I think you've made an excellent choice."

"Okay, but nobody can know. If he knows about my family...Even worse, if they know about him..." I shuddered at the thought. "Disaster."

"Aunt Eden?" My niece's voice jolted me and I whipped toward the top of the staircase.

"Hey, Olivia."

"Mom-mom says not to ruin dinner by coming down late." She cocked her head. "She also said to make sure you look presentable. Do you?"

I adjusted the hem of my top. "Of course I do."

Olivia scrunched her nose. "I'm not sure I would wear those shoes. They make your feet look big."

"My feet *are* big," I said.

Her blue eyes rounded. "Will my feet be that big when I grow up?"

"Hard to tell at this point," I said. "Your mom has petite feet, so maybe you'll take after her." Which I refused to resent because Verity couldn't help her perfect, dainty feet any more than I could help my clodhoppers.

"Great Nyx, I hope so," she breathed and disappeared down the steps.

I turned back to Alice. "You might want to go haunt the town for a couple of hours. Dinner is likely to make your head hurt even worse."

"You can't be serious, dear. I told you I'm looking for entertainment and you're about to endure a family dinner. I'll see you downstairs." She winked and then dissipated.

I descended the steps, humming *Fly Me to the Moon* again, and immediately ran into Tomas, Uncle Moyer's husband, as he returned from the bathroom. With his golden hair and laidback appeal, the angel-human hybrid was like a supernatural surfer.

"Eden, you darling fury." He greeted me with a kiss on each cheek. "I was hoping you'd be joining us this evening."

"How could I miss it?" Especially when my mother had threatened to hex me with a cold sore on my lip if I didn't show.

Everyone was standing around the island in the kitchen, nibbling on raw vegetables that I had no doubt Verity was responsible for. A veggie tray was far too wholesome for my mother.

"I don't see what the problem is," my mother was saying. "If I have a clear vision of how I'd like my funeral to go, why not carry out my wishes?"

Anton bristled. "I am not hiring *strippers* to *perform* at your funeral."

"Why ever not?" my mother asked. "You said it yourself—it's *my* funeral."

"And you will be dead, therefore, not in a position to enjoy the gyrating gentlemen you've requested," Anton said, rather reasonably.

Olivia tugged on her father's hand. "What's a stripper?"

"Later." Anton handed her a carrot stick and patted her on the head.

Verity bit a slice of red pepper in half. "I'd like my family and close friends to say a few kind words and then go back into the world feeling better for having known me."

My mother smiled. "Yes, that sounds every bit as boring as I imagined your funeral would be."

"I've decided I want a Viking funeral," Grandma announced. She set her phone on the island. "I still want the same playlist. Be sure to blast *Immigrant Song* for the finale."

Anton nodded. "No problem. We can do that from the marina."

"No problem?" I elbowed my brother in the ribs. "We cannot set Grandma on fire and push her out into the Chesapeake with heavy metal music blaring. We'd get arrested."

"Why?" he asked. "She'd already be dead, plus it's a good song."

"Thank you," Grandma said. "I figured it would liven things up. Block the sounds of your mother's wailing cries."

Aunt Thora removed a pan from the oven. "I would like to be cremated after my service and my ashes spread under a lemon tree in the yard."

"I don't know," my mother said, thinking. "Ashes might negatively impact the flavor."

Uncle Moyer took a sip of wine. "I've been privy to a good many funeral parties in my line of work. More than a few clients throw a party before they go, so they can enjoy it. When you know you've already sold your soul, you tend to spare no expense."

My mother clapped her hands together. "That's a wonderful idea, Moyer. I should throw myself a party."

"You do that most weekends and the occasional Wednesday," Grandma said.

I felt something brush against my shoe and looked down

to see Charlemagne slither past me. A shrimp had fallen on the floor and the python was heading straight for it. Unfortunately, Candy must've also spotted the shrimp and leaped down from the windowsill with a proprietary hiss. They reached the shrimp at the same time. Charlemagne stabbed one end with a fang and Candy bit down on the other end. Both refused to acquiesce and they each pulled, trying to force their opponent to let go. The black cat's tail swished in anger and frustration as she struggled to claim the whole shrimp. Finally, the shrimp snapped in half and the animals went flying backward. Candy slid into the kitchen cabinet next to the stove and hissed once she'd gobbled down the half a shrimp. Charlemagne, however, was longer and more unwieldy. The python's body was like a rubber band, snapping ankles as it shot backward. He made it as far as the coffee table, bouncing off and landing on the floor with a thud.

From a distant corner of the room, Alice laughed merrily. "I adore slapstick!"

I ignored the commotion and tried to focus on the conversation.

"What kind of funeral do I want?" Olivia asked. She looked at her mother with the kind of solemn, thoughtful expression that only young children seemed capable of, where the fate of the world rested on the answer to this single question.

"It's really not an appropriate conversation for children," Verity said. She sat at the table with Ryan while he shoveled handfuls of sliced grapes into his mouth.

"How is it not appropriate?" Grandma asked. "Death is an inevitable part of life. The yin to the yang. It's not helpful to pretend otherwise."

Olivia's lower lip began to tremble. "I don't want to die."

My mother bent over to comfort her. "There, there,

sweetheart. Only Aunt Eden is lucky enough not to die in this family. Not permanently, anyway. On the downside, that means there will be no one left to host a funeral for her."

The reality of the statement slammed into me. Hard.

"Eden, are you well?" Although I heard Tomas's voice, he sounded far away.

"I think she's in shock," Verity said. Their voices continued, sounding as though they were in a tunnel.

"Quick, someone fetch me a glass of lemonade," Aunt Thora urged.

"Quick, someone slap her," Grandma said.

A hand cracked against my cheek, jolting me back to the moment.

"Eden?" Aunt Thora thrust a cold glass into my hand. "Drink this. You'll feel better."

My mother flexed her hand. "I don't know about her, but I already feel better."

"Sorry, I don't know what happened," I said.

"I do," Tomas said, eyeing me sympathetically. "You fully grasped the repercussions of immortality."

I blinked rapidly. "I'd rather not think about it right now. Is dinner ready? I'm starving."

I made it through the main course by focusing on what I could control—the rate at which I chewed. How much I drank. I strained to listen to the sound that was farthest away, a trick I'd learned from Fergus during our FBI stakeouts. Tonight it was cicadas and, briefly, the rumble of a distant airplane. The noise was both calming and distracting. Maybe John wasn't wrong about his devotion to meditation.

I didn't want to think about immortality. I mean, I already knew I didn't want it. I didn't want any of my fury traits, no matter how desirable some of them were. I couldn't imagine who would covet my crown of snakes, though I had no doubt there was someone in the world that would.

As an immortal, every relationship I had would be temporary. Granted, that was true for everyone to a lesser degree, but for me—it was much worse. How could I dare to give my heart to Chief Fox when I might live dozens—even hundreds—of lifetimes after him? It was too much to contemplate.

Olivia leaned over and whispered, "Aunt Eden, you look sad."

"That's just her face," my mother interjected. "You'll get used to it, though it's nothing a little Botox and filler can't fix."

"Moyer can give you a referral," Aunt Thora said. "He goes every three months for Botox. Made a deal with a plastic surgeon."

"Mother!" Uncle Moyer gasped. "That's private information."

"I knew," Tomas said. "And you look incredible, by the way. No judgment."

Uncle Moyer planted a quick kiss on his husband's lips. "I'm sorry. I should have told you, but I was embarrassed. You're so effortlessly youthful and attractive."

"See? It all worked out," Aunt Thora said.

The doorbell rang and Princess Buttercup bolted for the front door, barking incessantly. I hadn't even realized she was downstairs until that moment.

Aunt Thora followed the hellhound to the door. She returned a minute later, her face pale and her body stiff. I didn't understand the issue until I saw the three women behind her.

"LeRoux," Grandma hissed. Candy joined her from the windowsill.

"We're not here to cause trouble, Esther," Adele said. "I apologize for interrupting your family time, but we have a situation."

She didn't need to say more for me to know that Rosalie was 'the situation.' The witch seemed off kilter, even for Rosalie. Her eyes couldn't seem to focus and she was muttering to herself.

"Colors," Rosalie murmured. "So many colors in one room. So bright."

Grandma rose to her feet. "I don't see how we can help."

"I'm not here for your help," Adele said. "I'm here for hers." She looked at Verity. "Your neighbor said you might be here."

Verity set down her fork. "Of course." Her gaze swept the room. "We need privacy."

"The attic," I said. "Bring her to my room." The space was untidy with clothes on the floor and the sheets in a bunch at the bottom of the mattress, but I doubted the witches would care about that right now.

I hurried ahead of them to lead the way. Adele and Corinne accompanied Rosalie, and Verity brought up the rear.

"No one else," I heard Verity say firmly. Good for her. The druid could be forceful when she had to be, which wasn't surprising. No way would my brother have married a weakling. He was too accustomed to strong women.

The witches sat Rosalie on my mattress.

"You don't even have a bed?" Corinne asked me.

"It's only temporary," I replied. "When I move into the barn, I'll get a real bed."

Her expression suggested that this was unacceptable, even temporarily, but whatever. It wasn't as though I'd expected to end up here.

"How can I help?" Verity asked.

"My daughter has been acting strangely," Adele said. "In fact, I'd mentioned it to Eden at the council meeting."

"You said she was disconnected from reality or something," I said.

"Yes," Adele said. She stroked the pearls around her neck. "It's getting worse. She keeps talking about seeing colors everywhere. You can't have a real conversation with her."

"Do you read auras?" Verity asked. "Maybe she's overstimulated on them?"

"I don't know," Adele said. "I can't seem to have a sensible conversation with her. Believe me, we've both tried."

"I asked her if she wanted dinner and she started ranting and raving about colors," Corinne said. "Then she kept shouting 'the red is too bright' over and over again."

Verity crouched down to address Rosalie. "Hi there, Rosalie. I'm not sure if you remember me, but I'm Dr. Verity. I'd like to examine you, if that's okay."

"You're not going to undress her, are you?" a voice asked. "Because I can't unsee that."

I whirled around. "Grandma! You don't need to see anything. You shouldn't even be up here."

"This is my house."

"No, this is technically my mother's house," I said.

"Go downstairs and stay there," Verity warned. Something in her tone made everyone sit up straight and pay attention.

"Fine," Grandma huffed, "but you'd better not be leaving any curses behind." She stomped back downstairs.

"Ignore her," I said.

"I'd like a few minutes alone with Rosalie, if that's okay," Verity said.

I guided Adele and Corinne to the kitchen where Aunt Thora offered them a plate of food.

"No thank you," Adele said. "I'm much too anxious to eat."

"We haven't poisoned it," Grandma said. "Though there was a quick discussion about it."

"Grandma, please," I said. "They're our guests. Let's make them feel welcome."

"Fine," Grandma said. "We're discussing our funeral preferences. What would you like, Adele? I'd be happy to help with the arrangements."

To her credit, the witch took the question in stride. "Something tasteful and elegant. A brunch with a champagne toast."

"That sounds lovely," Corinne said.

"Background music," Adele continued. "Not too brash. Something like the song you were humming at our meeting, Eden." She began to hum *Fly Me to the Moon*.

"You've been humming that a lot lately," my mother said. "I heard you in the shower."

"Frank Sinatra," Uncle Moyer said approvingly. "I'm surprised you know his work."

"It's called YouTube," I said. I wasn't about to credit Chief Fox.

Verity appeared in the kitchen with Rosalie. "Can I see you witches in private?" She escorted Rosalie to the door and Adele and Corinne followed.

I returned to the table for more food, anxiously awaiting the diagnosis. Verity came back alone a few minutes later.

"Is she sick, Mommy?" Olivia asked. "Will we need to plan her funeral?"

Verity ruffled her daughter's hair. "Not at all, sweetheart. She just needs rest and a calm environment."

"Well, that rules out staying here," Anton said.

Verity passed the potatoes. "I've seen a few patients like her this week. Delusional. Disconnected. I recommended a potion that Adele can make at home. If that doesn't help, then we'll have to move on to the next step."

"What's the next step?" I asked.

"There are places that will look after witches in Rosalie's condition," Verity said matter-of-factly.

"A supernatural psych ward?" I asked, aghast.

"I always knew she was crazy," my mother said. "It was only a matter of time."

I chewed my potatoes in stunned silence. With everything else going on in Chipping Cheddar right now, I wasn't so sure. Rosalie's situation was far worse than an irritable Paul Masterson or wayward Father Kevin, though. It was time to kick this investigation into high gear.

CHAPTER ELEVEN

I STRUGGLED to open the door to my office so as not to spill my coffee. In the end, it was like fighting my way through a wind tunnel and I ended up with a scrape on my arm and a splash of coffee on my white T-shirt.

"That problem could have been easily avoided by setting the cup down in order to open the door," Neville said. He stood at the table in the back of the room, hunched over an object I couldn't see.

"You look busy," I said. I dropped my bag onto my desk and proceeded to the back of the room to be nosy. "What are you working on?"

"Mrs. Huntington's issue with the wolves," he said. "I'm creating a device that can be used to detect whether werewolves are, indeed, violating her garden."

"Isn't that just called a surveillance camera?"

Neville clucked his tongue. "O ye of little magical knowledge. This device will be much more effective. A human security camera will only confirm the existence of a wolf. My device will also identify which werewolf it is, as long as it's someone resident in Chipping Cheddar. I've programmed it with a roster of every werewolf in town."

"Even Julie and Meg?" I asked. Not that either one of them would be responsible. They took a potion once a month to avoid shifting.

"I have to be comprehensive," Neville said.

I drank my coffee, observing his handiwork. The device was the size of a cufflink. "Where will you put it?"

"You said it's the side garden, yes? I'll affix it to the house just above the garden. Mrs. Huntington won't even know it's there."

"Her cats will probably tell her."

He smiled and continued tinkering. "If this works as it should, we should be able to identify the culprit and handle the situation quietly."

"You're an absolute treasure, Neville."

He bowed his head. "I live to serve, O infernal one."

"Good, because we seem to have a more serious situation on our hands."

Neville's head jerked to attention. "More serious than a disgruntled gnome?"

"Rosalie LeRoux." I filled him in on Verity's diagnosis. "I think it's connected to some of the other issues that have cropped up this week."

"But it sounds as though Rosalie is suffering a psychotic break," Neville said. "There are physical symptoms as well. Father Kevin simply wants to change careers."

"Julie," I said. "She was also acting out of character. I thought it was some kind of reverse psychology, but now I'm not so sure." My thoughts turned to my mother and her... issue. "Oh no."

"What is it?" Neville asked.

"I don't think it's another chaos demon, but there's definitely a supernatural influence at work." Aunt Thora had been right all along, and here I'd only been trying to placate her. Come to think of it, even Aunt Thora had been acting out of character lately, oversharing and revealing secrets.

"How can I help?" Neville asked, ever the good assistant.

A knock at the door startled both of us. We weren't exactly used to visitors dropping by the office. Most people in town thought that we sat at a computer checking for hackers.

I opened the door to reveal Chief Fox. I could tell by the expression on his face that it wasn't a social call. "What's wrong?"

"I need to talk to you."

My heart thumped. Did he know about my family? Was he here to tell me it was over and that he was turning me in for harboring supernatural criminals?

I stepped aside. "Do you want to come in? You look...unhappy."

He shook his head. "I need you to come with me. It's Mayor Whitehead."

My spirits lifted. Not my family after all. Rejoice! "Is she hurt?"

"No, but she might be if she keeps this up," the chief said cryptically. "People are getting pissed off."

Uh oh.

"Am I needed?" Neville called. "I'd like to finish my device and get it set up."

Chief Fox looked at me. "Should I ask?"

I shook my head. "It's a werewolf thing." I glanced over my shoulder. "I'll catch up with you later, Neville."

"I'll drive," the chief offered.

I hopped into the passenger seat. "No Achilles?"

"No, I didn't want to put him in an uncomfortable situation. The mayor is usually so reasonable. This is..."

"Out of character?"

He looked at me sideways as he drove. "Yeah." He paused. "Something I need to know, Agent Fury?"

"Something's going on and it's probably supernatural," I said.

"That's nice and vague."

I shrugged. "Right now it's all I've got."

"So I shouldn't judge the mayor too harshly for this?"

"I wouldn't."

As we pulled alongside the curb, I second-guessed myself. The first thing I noticed was a large sign with handprinted letters—This spot reserved for Mayor Whitehead. Violators will be towed at their own expense. The parking spot itself was blocked by three orange cones. Deputy Guthrie stood sentry, seemingly there to ward off those who would dare park there.

"Why is Sean there?" I asked.

"She ordered him to guard her spot and make sure no one parked there," the chief said. "He told her that the cones and the sign were probably sufficient, but she yelled at him and threatened to take his badge if he didn't comply."

"And he called you?"

"Sure did, along with five other residents who overheard the commotion. She did it outside in front of her office."

We left the car and approached the deputy, who looked less than thrilled to be spending his day guarding a parking spot.

"Hey, Sean. Should we get you one of those beefeater hats?" I asked.

He scowled at me. "You said you were getting help, Chief."

"Agent Fury *is* help," Chief Fox replied. "The mayor likes her."

"Hard to imagine why," Deputy Guthrie muttered.

The mayor pulled beside us and rolled down her window.

"You can move those cones, Deputy. I'll be parking now. I'm meeting a friend for coffee on the beach."

Chief Fox and I stepped aside to give her room to maneuver into the spot. Mayor Whitehead popped open the door and a slender leg appeared, followed by another. She beamed when she noticed us.

"How do you like my sign?" she asked, tinkling with laughter.

"I heard the council voted against a designated waterfront spot for you," I said.

The mayor scowled. "And I overrode their veto, which is well within my rights as mayor of this town."

"You don't see it as an abuse of power?" I asked. It was probably useless to engage in this conversation right now. If there was a supernatural force at work, it was doubtful she'd listen to reason.

The mayor looked me up and down. "Listen Agent Fury, I appreciate your interest, but I can assure you that securing this spot for my own personal use is entirely ethical." She slung a handbag over her shoulder and started to walk away.

"Aren't you going to put money in?" the chief asked, pointing to the blinking meter.

Mayor Whitehead tossed her head back and laughed. "I'm the mayor, darling. I think I've earned free parking in this town, don't you?"

"I'm the chief of police, but I don't think for one second that I've earned anything," he said.

From the sidelines, Deputy Guthrie watched the scene unfold with interest.

"You're still new to Chipping Cheddar, Chief Fox," she said. She patted his cheek in a condescending gesture. "You'll come around." She spun around and walked away, her heels clicking on the pavement.

"I hope she takes off those shoes before she hits the beach or she'll get stuck in the sand," I said.

"In that case, I hope she keeps them on," the chief said under his breath.

"What's gotten into her?" Deputy Guthrie asked. He was so distracted by the mayor that he didn't bother to insult me.

"It's temporary, Guthrie," the chief said. He clapped the deputy on the shoulder. "Trust me, it'll work out soon enough. Isn't that right, Agent Fury?"

"I sure hope so or we're going to have to hold an early election," I said. The residents of Chipping Cheddar weren't going to tolerate a mayor that abused her position. "Let's try to keep this quiet for now." I knew I could count on Husbourne to persuade the other town council members to keep mum on the subject. Nobody wanted a scandal.

"What am I supposed to do?" Deputy Guthrie asked. "Wait here until she's finished so that I can put the cones back?"

Part of me wanted to say yes, only so that I could torture Sean. The more mature part of me shook my head. "And if she calls you, don't answer."

He shot a quizzical look at the chief. "Really?"

"Whatever Agent Fury says goes," the chief replied. "She's the expert."

"On annoying women?" Deputy Guthrie asked. "I guess I can see that."

I narrowed my eyes at the redhead. "Careful, Sean, or I'll have you working as a parking attendant for every public official in this town."

The deputy shot an aggrieved looked at his boss, but Chief Fox only chuckled in response. "Good luck, Deputy."

When I got back in the car, I noticed the time. "Would you mind dropping me off at the diner? I have a lunch date with Clara."

"You don't think you should cancel?"

"If it were anyone else I would, but Clara is good to bounce ideas off of," I said.

"How about me?" the chief asked.

I smiled. "I'd like to bounce a lot of things off you, but right now Clara has more experience with the supernatural realm, so she's my better option."

He drummed his fingers on the steering wheel. "Now my imagination is running away with me. I'm picturing a lot of bouncing."

I offered a peck on the cheek before I vacated the car, careful to check that no one was watching. I hurried into Gouda Nuff where Clara was already seated in our usual booth.

"Sorry I'm late," I said. "My official presence was required." I noticed a plate of cheese quesadillas in the middle and two iced teas. "Thanks for ordering."

"I was hungry."

I gobbled down a triangle of quesadilla as I explained the situation with Mayor Whitehead.

Clara seemed unconcerned. "She's the mayor. Why shouldn't she be cut some slack?"

I gaped at my best friend. "Clara Riley, I can't believe you just said that. She's not above the law any more than I am."

"You think everything should be so black and white all the time," she said, "but you're willing to bend your own moral code when it suits you."

I reeled back. "What are you talking about?"

"You're lying to everyone about Chief Fox and, even worse, you're making him lie too."

Heat crept up the back of my neck. "You know why I have to do that."

"Because your family is evil." She rolled her eyes. "Need I mention that you tore Mrs. Hughes's yoga pants in front of the whole class? Not exactly a decision I'd catalogue under 'good.'"

Now my whole face was red. "How do you even know about that? You left before I did."

"Someone mentioned it and I put two and two together."

"It was a little prank and she deserved it. You know how awful she is."

For someone willing to cut the mayor slack, Clara seemed incapable of cutting me any. "Maybe you and your family meet in the middle more than you think," she said. "I mean, when's the last time they really hurt anyone? Do you even know?"

"That's the only measure of evil now? Pain and suffering?" I knew for a fact that my father was still working as a full-time vengeance demon. Our tacit agreement was that he didn't take jobs in my territory and didn't offer any details so that I could remain blissfully ignorant.

"Your mother and grandmother seem to spend more time killing each other than hurting anyone else," Clara said.

"Even if that's true, that doesn't absolve them of years of bad behavior," I said. "Besides, they still use black magic. They just make an effort to hide it from me."

"And why do you think they do that?"

"Because they don't want to get caught," I said. "They don't want me to turn them in."

Clara made a dismissive noise at the back of her throat. "You think it's self-preservation."

"Of course. Their motivations are purely selfish."

Clara fixed me with a hard stare. "So selfish that they've gifted you the barn on their property so you can have your own place to live?"

"Trust me. That's a selfish move. They want me under

their thumb so they can torture me and the best way to achieve that is to make me an offer I'd be a fool to refuse."

Clara leaned back against the chair and observed me coolly. "You get so worked up about them putting you in a box that you haven't noticed that you've done the same to them."

"Even if you're right—and I'm not saying that you are—a good deed for one person doesn't negate being horrible to everyone else. Grandma wouldn't hesitate to hex half the senior center if she thought she could get away with it. Ever since she claims they cheated during Mahjong, she's been itching for revenge."

Clara splayed her hands on the table. "This argument is tiresome and I have another boring article to write."

"What's it about?"

"A cat saved its owner by calling 9-1-1 when she fell down the steps."

My eyes popped. "How is that boring? Clara, that's a wonderful story." I made a mental note to teach Princess Buttercup how to use my phone. Then again, her acidic slobber would probably short circuit the connection.

"Whatever. The woman's like ninety. The cat didn't do her any favors by extending her miserable life."

I'd never heard such harsh words come out of my friend's mouth. "Clara, this isn't you." She sounded so heartless—the opposite of the Clara I knew.

"I'm tired of giving a flying rat's butt about everyone else's feelings. Where has that gotten me? I can't even move up the ladder at *The Buttermilk Bugle*, the most podunk newspaper in the history of podunk newspapers." She pulled a long, thin wrapper out of her purse.

"That's a plastic straw," I said.

"No kidding," she snapped. "I don't want to use a paper

one. They disintegrate before I even finish my drink. The environment can suck it."

Great Nyx, I hated to ask my next question. "Is this PMS talking?"

Clara barked a short laugh. "I have an epiphany about the state of the world and my place in it and you want to blame PMS?" She grunted. "And you call yourself a feminist. Take a hard look in the mirror, Eden. You're not the Jedi you'd like to believe and your family isn't on the dark side."

"Members of the Sith Order," I corrected her.

Clara gave her head a shake. "Not really the point." She tore off the wrapper and shoved the straw into the cup of ice water. "Maybe we shouldn't have reconnected when you came back to town."

My chest squeezed. "You can't mean that."

"To be honest, I don't know that our friendship is worth the aggravation."

The pressure of tears began to build behind my eyes. "Clara, I'm sorry if I said something to upset you..."

She sucked the rest of her drink through the straw and stood. "I'll see you around, Eden."

I watched her go, unable to move or speak. This was so much worse than the last time our friendship had hit the skids. That had been me, trying to distance myself from Chipping Cheddar and my family. Clearly, that had worked out well for me.

The waitress approached the table. "Should I bring the check? Sorry, I didn't realize you two were finished."

I nodded, afraid that if I opened my mouth, I'd unleash a torrent of tears. I didn't realize we were finished either, but it seemed glaringly obvious now.

CHAPTER TWELVE

"Are you ready?" Neville stood hunched over with his hands on his knees.

"We're not playing catch," I said. "Stand up and look alert."

Neville straightened. "Sorry, kettle. I couldn't hear you over your rounded shoulders and weak core."

I gasped. "Don't you dare." I swung my long, dark hair over my shoulder. "I'll have you know I have been making a valiant effort to strengthen my core and improve my posture."

"So you're basically admitting that nagging works. Parents everywhere will rejoice at the news."

"I'm saying no such thing." I raised my chin in defiance. "Maybe you should consider yoga. It might help you learn how to stand properly." I motioned to his awkwardly posed body.

Neville huffed. "How is it that you'd like me to stand, Agent Fury?"

"I don't know. Try a position that doesn't make you look ready to sit on the toilet."

Neville's cheeks were tinged with pink. "Why don't we start with strength training?"

"Will it involve breaking a sweat? Because I have plans to see Chief Fox later."

"There's this magical invention called a shower," Neville said.

"Then I have to go home first," I said. "I'm trying to avoid that for obvious reasons."

Neville's brow creased. "You don't intend to change your clothes?"

I glanced down at my pale green T-shirt and shorts. "What's wrong with this?"

"The cat on your shirt looks like it's been flattened by some unseen force and the message reads 'not today.'" Neville pinched the bridge of his nose. "Please tell me why that's the message you'd want to send to the chief on your date."

I shrugged. "It's unintentionally accurate. He's not getting lucky today, no matter how many fruity cocktails he buys for me. It will take at least a steak dinner at Chophouse and we can't go there because of Rafael."

Neville closed his eyes. "TMI, Agent Fury."

"I'm kidding about the steak." Sort of. "You should get out there, Neville. Try to meet someone. It can't be fulfilling to spend all your time with me."

"Perhaps when I feel you're completely up to speed…"

"How am I not up to speed?" I asked.

Neville waved his hands in the air. "We're in the middle of Davenport Park for a training exercise. Do you think I spent time doing this with Agent Pidcock?"

"No, I think you two spent time braiding each other's hair and watching paint dry because there was nothing else to do."

Neville pressed his lips together, appearing to fight the urge to say more. "Strength training exercise number one."

I wiggled my fingers. "Lay it on me, Wyman." I needed to blow off some steam after my argument with Clara. I'd been so upset at the time, it was only later when I reflected on it that I realized Clara was likely under the same supernatural influence as the mayor and countless others. Clara Riley was the most compassionate person I knew and there was no way her heart had grown so hard that she would turn her nose up at a heroic cat story.

The wizard pulled a wand from his pocket and pointed at me. The tip of his wand sparked with orange light and, the next thing I knew, an enormous spider knocked me to the ground. Its body pressed down on me, pinning me to the ground, while its legs flailed around me. I tried to yell, but there was too much weight on my chest. I could hardly breathe, let alone speak.

I tried not to panic and focused on the weight rather than the nuclear radiation-style spider that Neville decided to conjure. This was punishment for criticizing his posture. And here I thought only my family was capable of being petty. How silly of me.

I wriggled my body so that my left arm was on the edge of the spider's body, where the weight wasn't as heavy. I'd always been strong—my mother loved any excuse to hand me a jar, though she preferred to attribute my strength to my large, manly hands. I'd had to tone down my abilities during FBI training and act weaker than I was. I deserved an Oscar for that performance. On the other hand, the more often I used my powers, the more the gods gave me, so I had no qualms about pretending to be a normal woman. These exercises didn't concern me because I knew it would take quite a number of heavy spiders over a period of time to trigger another fury trait. They weren't the equivalent of—you know—killing myself.

"Stop squirming so I can eat you," the spider said. "I haven't had my dinner yet."

Great balls of fury! Neville made it talk? Ugh.

I tried to push, but I needed more leverage. I inched over a little more and cupped my left hand around the side of the spider's body.

"Stop. That tickles," the spider complained.

"Fine," I ground out. "I'll stop." I pushed as hard as I could and the spider flipped onto its back. Its legs dangled in the air as it tried to correct its position.

"Well done, Agent Fury," Neville said.

I scrambled to my feet and wiped the spider residue off my body. "When I pictured a nice warm body on top of me, that wasn't the scenario I had in mind, Neville."

"Sorry to disappoint you. Next time I'll conjure a more attractive demon so that you can practice your tonsil hockey before you heave him off."

I shuddered at the thought. "Now I definitely need a shower," I said.

As Neville waved his wand and made the spider disappear, a beeping sound made my heart skip a beat.

"Did you set an alarm?" I asked.

He patted his pockets. "It's the surveillance device at Mrs. Huntington's." He pulled a gadget from his pocket that was the size of a watch and looked at it. "Ladies and gentlemen, we have ourselves a werewolf."

I hurried to his side for a better view. "Can you see who it is?"

"The system is scanning for a match now." Lights blinked around the face of the gadget as it worked to identify the werewolf on the tiny screen. I recognized the dead flowers in the patch of garden at Mrs. Huntington's house.

The lights stopped blinking and the image of the werewolf was replaced by a name—Jarvis Lightfoot.

"Neville, you're a genius!" I punched his arm.

"Ouch!" he cried and rubbed his arm. "If you're going to hit me, get out of strength training mode first."

"Sorry," I said. "I'm going to head over there now and stalk him."

"Is that wise, Agent Fury? Perhaps wait until he goes home and returns to his human form."

"I'll be fine, Neville. He's peeing on flowers, not robbing a bank at gunpoint. Let's keep this in perspective."

"He's murdering living things."

"Okay, now you sound like Mrs. Huntington." I started toward the street where my car was parked. "I'll update you when I know something."

In the end, I decided to drive to Jarvis Lightfoot's house instead, not that I would give Neville the satisfaction of knowing that I heeded his advice. A quick Google search directed me to his house on Provolone Lane. The interior lights of the house were off, so I parked in the driveway and sat on the stoop, waiting for him to return. Without thinking, I found myself playing on Little Critters. I'd installed the app on my phone because of Grandma, but I had to admit it was addictive, despite the fact that I had no idea what I was doing. I quickly learned that if I tapped the screen often enough, I did something right.

"Can I help you with something?"

I glanced up to see a scrawny young man with disheveled brown hair. He was bare-chested and his jeans were a little too baggy, showing off the waistband of his boxers.

"Are you Jarvis Lightfoot?"

He frowned. "Who's asking?"

"I'm Agent Eden Fury." I produced my badge and held it up for inspection.

Jarvis leaned forward to study the badge. "Federal Bureau of Magic? Well, ain't you special."

"Jarvis, are you aware that public urination is a misdemeanor punishable by a fine or jail time?"

His body tensed. "I don't know what you're talking about."

I stood so that we were at eye level. "You've been shifting into your wolf form and giving Mrs. Huntington's garden a golden shower."

He grimaced. "No way, man. Do you even know what a golden shower is?"

Although Grandma was the expert on urban dictionary terms, somehow, I knew this was one I should research on my own. "You've been peeing on her flowers and killing them. She's very upset."

"What makes you think it's me? There are dozens of werewolves in this town."

"They don't all shift and you were the only one caught on surveillance." I offered a triumphant smile.

His smug expression crumpled. "You recorded me?"

"'Fraid so. Can you explain why you've been targeting her garden?"

Jarvis raked a hand through his messy hair, making it even worse. "I've been…not myself lately."

"What do you mean?"

"I don't normally shift this much," he said. "Once a month, maybe. Sometimes not even that."

"Why the change?"

"I don't know." He seemed genuinely puzzled. "I just feel like it so, when the mood strikes, I do it."

"And that's unusual for you?"

"It is when it's like this," Jarvis said. "I'll be in the middle of a project and feel like shifting. The other day I was fixing the kitchen sink and felt like shifting, so I left the whole mess and went running through the woods howling like some kind of animal."

I squinted at him. "You *are* some kind of animal."

He leaned a hand on the railing of the stoop. "I can't explain it. I feel unsettled until I shift. Then I'm cool again for a little while until the pressure builds back up."

"Why do you go to that particular place to…do your business?"

"I just follow the scent of where others have gone before me," he said. "I know one of my buddies has urinated there before because he knows that old gnome hates our kind. I think I go there instinctively."

Okay, so it seemed the shifting itself was more of an issue than the destination.

"Have you changed medications lately? Started a new one?"

Jarvis shook his head. "I don't take nothin,' not even vitamins."

"Any stressful issues in your personal or professional life?" Sometimes a breakup or a job change could trigger a shifter's need to get in touch with his primal side.

"Nope. Ain't been dating nobody and job's the same as it's always been. It's a real drag, but that ain't new."

"Can you think of anything unusual that might have happened to you recently?"

He hiked up his jeans. "Nope. Pretty boring, really. Maybe that's why I've been shifting more. Trying to make up for how bored I am."

"It's possible, but it seems more like an itch you need to scratch than a conscious choice." I tilted my head, studying him. "Run me through your last few days. Any chance you were near the marina?"

"There's every chance," he said. "That's where I work. I'm a boat mechanic"

"Huh." It seemed that whatever was affecting certain residents might also be affecting Jarvis Lightfoot. "Do you know Judy and Paul Masterson?"

He brightened. "Sure do. They keep their boat at the marina. *Last Ark*."

"Have you seen them in the past few days?"

"Nope. I only see them if they need something for the boat."

"Were you on their boat at all?" I was grasping at straws, but there had to be a connection. I felt it in my bones.

"Not in a few weeks." He gestured to his front door. "Is that it? I'd like a shower. I always stink after I shift."

"That's it for now," I said. "Do me a favor though—if you shift again, stay off Mrs. Huntington's property. Just keep to the woods."

He saluted me. "Yes, ma'am." He started to move past me on the stoop. "You kind of smell. You sure you don't want to shower? I'll wash your back if you wash mine."

"No thanks, Jarvis." Guys like this baffled me. At no point during our conversation did I express a personal interest in him, yet he still felt perfectly at ease propositioning me. It had to be a matter of odds—the more often he tried this approach, the more likely that eventually some woman would agree.

"Your loss," he said, and opened the front door.

"I saw the surveillance footage, Jarvis," I reminded him. "I feel fairly confident that I'm not missing out."

The door slammed behind him and I sauntered back to my car with a satisfied smile.

CHAPTER THIRTEEN

"I DIDN'T REALIZE you had a boat here," I said. I boarded the sleek Sea Ray at the marina for my clandestine date with the chief. I handed him the cooler I'd packed.

"How could I resist when I live right on the water?" he said. "Some of my favorite memories involve being on the water. I figured why not make more?" He wrapped his arms around my waist and nuzzled my neck. His warm breath on my neck made my body tingle.

"We should probably keep our hands to ourselves or someone might see us," I said.

"Right. Operation Top Secret. Sorry." I felt his reluctance as he released me. "I guess that means no sleepover on the boat tonight."

"That's a definite no. If I didn't come home to the attic, my mother would send out her winged monkeys to find me."

He chuckled. "Does she really have winged monkeys? I'm not sure what's a joke anymore."

"They're real," I said, "but she doesn't actually have any." I sat on the leather seat closest to him and let the chief play captain. He settled into the captain's chair like a king ascending the throne—he was a natural. Watching him take command of the boat was unexpectedly appealing. I was accustomed to being the active one—the one to take charge or issue orders. This was a nice change of pace.

He skillfully maneuvered the boat out of the marina and into the bay. As we picked up speed, I enjoyed the wind in my hair and the scenery rushing by. I wished we could spend time together like this every day. I tried not to dwell on the negative and focus on the fact that we were on a date. A real date with food and sunsets and hopefully kissing. Once we reached his desired location, the chief dropped anchor and grinned at me.

"This is nice," I said.

He bent down and kissed me. "We should probably eat first."

"First implies something comes after," I said.

"Something does," he said with a suggestive wink. "Dessert." He pointed to the sky. "Let's wait until sunset though. It's too pretty to do anything else right now except enjoy it."

"Nature's art," I said.

We moved to the seats at the back of the boat so that we could snuggle together in comfortable silence. Ribbons of pink and orange streaked across the sky.

"There's no place I'd rather be right now," he said quietly.

Although I felt the same way, the words got stuck in my throat. Chief Fox didn't seem bothered by my failure to respond. His lips grazed my cheek as the sun finally dipped below the horizon.

"Showtime's over," he said. "That was something special, though."

"Do you have sunsets like that in Iowa?"

"I've seen beautiful lake sunsets," he said. "I especially love when the reflection ripples across the water. Never had company as beautiful as tonight to enjoy it with though."

"Well, that's a lie. I met your ex-girlfriend, remember?"

His sea-colored eyes drank me in. "She didn't hold a Yankee candle to you."

"What about a Nest candle? Did she hold one of those?"

He chuckled. "Don't know that brand so I can't comment."

"Time for the picnic?" I asked.

"Can it be called a picnic at this hour?" he asked.

"Of course."

I opened the cooler and produced two wrapped turkey and cheese sandwiches on torpedo rolls.

"Next time I'm taking you somewhere nice, like Chophouse," he said.

"No," I said quickly. "We can't go there." Definitely not there.

"No, I guess not." He took a thoughtful bite of the sandwich. "Explain to me again why we have to date in secret?"

I struggled for a good reason. "I just don't think people should know about us. They'll consider it a conflict of interest."

"The police chief and an FBI agent? Why would that be an issue?"

"It's in the FBM handbook," I said.

His mouth twitched into a smile. "Yes, but the average resident doesn't know about the FBM and I'm sure Neville will cut us some slack."

"Neville is the prickliest rule follower you'll ever meet," I said. "And you can't tell Sean. He'll be too happy to ruin everything for me."

"I have no intention of sharing details of my personal life with Deputy Guthrie. You have my word on that."

"Good."

The chief rubbed his jawline which brought my attention to his chin. I swore he did it on purpose because he knew how sexy I found that dimple.

"It sounds like we need to make a list of people allowed to know," he said. He wolfed down the remainder of his sandwich and I was suddenly glad I'd packed extra.

"That sounds extreme. How about we just don't tell anyone? Problem solved."

He eyed me curiously. "You're not going to tell Clara? Isn't she your best friend?"

"Clara knows," I mumbled. I shoved the rest of my sandwich into my mouth to avoid saying more. Now I felt like a hypocrite.

"Anyone else?" he asked.

"Sassy and Neville, but that's it." I didn't feel the need to mention Alice since the ghost wasn't a liability.

He clasped my hands in his. "Look, Fury, I'll be honest. I'm not a big fan of secrets. They tend to cause more trouble than they're meant to prevent."

"But you'll make an exception in this case, right?" I asked hopefully. Otherwise, this relationship was going to have to stop before it really started. I couldn't put him at risk.

He leaned his forehead against mine. "I understand the need for privacy. I just don't like it."

"There's another sandwich if you're still hungry," I said.

His eyes sparked with desire. "Oh, I'm still hungry."

My fingers slid through his thick hair as his lips crushed mine. If I had to sneak around on a boat with him for the next ten years, it would be worth it for a taste of his salty lips.

The sound of music broke us apart. I turned to see a smaller boat heading our way. As it drew closer, I noticed the name *Second Chance* painted on the side in black scripted letters.

"Beautiful evening," the older man on the boat yelled.

"Certainly is," Chief Fox replied.

I peered into the darkness. "Isn't that the groom from the party bus?"

"Hank," the chief said.

I gave him a quick look. "You're good at remembering names."

He grinned. "Part of the job."

Hank seemed to see us more clearly now. "Hey, there. I remember you two! The chief and the agent."

I shrank back. The whole point of being on the water was to avoid being seen together. At least Hank didn't travel in the same circles as anyone in my family.

"We're running a confidential investigation," I lied, "so we'd appreciate your discretion."

"No problem," Hank said, and saluted us.

A woman emerged from the shadows and slipped her hand into his. She looked close to his age with white hair and a deeply lined face. She wore a poppy-colored dress over her swimsuit.

"You must Jana," the chief said. "How was the wedding?"

Mother of hellhounds. The chief really was good with names.

"It was perfect." Hank pulled the woman in for a tight hug and smacked his lips against her cheek. "Isn't she beautiful? I'm the luckiest man in Chipping Cheddar."

"And I'm the luckiest woman." Jana smiled adoringly at her husband. It was clear they were very much in love.

"Why don't you have a drink with us?" Hank asked. "We have a bottle of champagne."

"Still celebrating, huh?" the chief asked.

"Hard to stop when you get to wake up next to this one every morning," Hank said. He kissed her again. I'd never seen an older man so effusive about his wife.

"It'll be a tight squeeze, but we can manage," the woman said.

"You're welcome to board our boat instead," the chief said. "We have plenty of space."

"You sure do," Hank said. "That's a nice boat."

"Thanks," the chief said.

I took a seat while Hank lined up his boat with ours and the chief helped the couple aboard.

"Did you catch the sunset?" Hank asked. "It was spectacular."

The cork was already popped so Hank poured the bubbling liquid into the plastic cups provided by Jana.

"Maybe just one more glass for you," Jana said quietly to her husband.

"I'll be fine," he insisted.

"The doctor said he should take it easy," Jana explained. "His blood pressure was a little high during his last visit."

"It was the stress of the wedding, but that's all over now," Hank said. "Now I can just enjoy the rest of my life with this beauty." He tipped back his cup and drained the champagne like it was water.

"Congratulations to both of you," I said. "Is this your first marriage, Jana?"

"No, but I've been divorced for over twenty years," she said. "Hank and I are all about second chances." She rubbed his stomach with affection.

"I wish I was young again," Hank said. "Then I'd have more time and energy for this spry thing." He gave his wife a playful spank and she nearly spilled her champagne.

"Ever been married?" Jana asked.

"No," the chief and I replied in unison.

"Don't wait too long or you'll miss out," Hank said. "You'll miss out on everything if you just watch from the sidelines."

"Young at heart," the chief commented. "I like it."

Hank set down the empty cup. "How about we skinny dip? I haven't done that in over fifty years and I honestly don't know what's holding me back." Without waiting for a response, Hank began to strip off his clothes.

"Hank," Jana said warily. "I don't know that it's such a good idea."

"Don't worry, Jana. You know I'll only have eyes for you." The striped boxers were the last to go before Hank jumped overboard.

"Cannonball!" he yelled, followed by a splash.

I ran to the edge of the boat and peered into the dark water. "Hank!" Sweat coated my palms. Before I could kick off my shoes to jump in after him, a blur shot past me and Chief Fox dove headfirst into the water.

"Hank!" Jana called. Her voice was frantic now. "How could he be so careless? He's not twenty anymore."

I couldn't look at her—couldn't even breathe. My gaze was fixed firmly on the water below. After a heart-stopping moment, the chief's head bobbed to the surface, followed by Hank's.

"Thank goodness," Jana breathed.

From the way Hank's head lolled to the side, I knew he was unconscious. The chief swam with one arm supporting Hank's body, making certain to keep the old man's head above the water.

I climbed down the ladder at the back of the boat. "I can pull him up," I said. Jana would be too distracted by Hank's current condition to notice my unusual display of strength.

The chief turned so that Hank was in front of him and I was able to pull him to safety. I immediately began CPR, but Hank remained unconscious. Chief Fox kneeled beside me, dripping pools of water.

"He needs a hospital," I said.

Behind us, Jana whimpered. "Is he okay? Please tell me he's okay."

I craned my neck to see her. "He's not responsive, Jana, but we're going to get him to a hospital as quickly as we can."

The older woman's body went limp and she promptly fainted. Thanks to my unnatural speed, I managed to catch her before she hit the deck.

Terrific. Now we had two unconscious people on the boat. This date was quickly becoming a disaster. It was probably punishment for my secrecy.

I released Jana and let her roll gently onto the deck.

"Is she okay?" the chief asked.

"She fainted, but she'll be fine in a minute." Which meant I only had a minute to help Hank before she recovered. "Close your eyes," I said, rising to a standing position.

The chief looked at me, his face rippled with confusion. "What do you mean?"

"I mean close your eyes. We're too far from land. The fastest way to get him help is to fly him there. You can get Jana to shore on the boat and drive her to the hospital. Make up a story as to how we got ahead of you."

"Why do I need to close my eyes? Is this about your wings?"

"I'd rather you not see them." Unfortunately, I wasn't wearing the invisibility locket that Neville had created for me. I needed to start wearing it on a daily basis in case of an emergency like this one. At least I'd be camouflaged in the evening. With my dark wings and dark hair, I'd blend into the gloaming.

"I've already seen them, remember?" he said.

"And I don't want to remind you how ugly I really am. Please, Sawyer. There isn't time to argue."

Thankfully, he didn't. The moment he squeezed his eyes

closed, I spread my wings, scooped a naked and unconscious Hank off the deck, and launched into the air.

An hour later the chief and I sat in the waiting room of the hospital while Jana lingered at her husband's bedside. Apparently, Hank had suffered a heart attack when he'd plunged into the water. We'd decided to wait with Jana until her daughter arrived from Baltimore.

"I'm going to check and see if she needs anything," I said. I rose to my feet and walked down the corridor to Hank's room. "How are you doing, Jana? Can I get you anything?"

Jana sat beside him, clutching his wrinkled hand. "I can't think about food right now. All I can think about is Hank."

I moved closer to her and placed a comforting hand on her shoulder. "The doctor said that Hank is strong and healthy for his age. There's a good chance he'll make a full recovery."

Tears streamed down Jana's cheeks. "I waited so long for us to be together. I can't bear the thought of losing him now."

"Didn't Hank's wife die two years ago?" I asked. That was what Chip had said on the party bus.

Jana wiped away a tear. "Yes, but I knew Hank long before that. I've always had feelings for him, but I kept a respectful distance from him because of his marriage. When we reconnected after she died, I thought I was finally being rewarded for all the good deeds I'd done in my life." She brought his hand to her lips. "I can't lose him. I just can't."

"The two of you seem very happy together," I said.

"Oh, it's been blissful. I admit it, he's been excitable lately, but I thought it was euphoria over our wedding. Now I'm not so sure."

My heart hammered in my chest. "Would you say he's been acting out of character?"

Jana twisted to look at me. "Not exactly out of character for Hank. More like too much of Hank. Normally he knows when to draw the line." She turned back to observe her husband. "Lately he only seems capable of dancing over it."

Whatever was happening in Chipping Cheddar, it was now abundantly clear that Hank was a victim too. Fear flooded my system. If I didn't get to the bottom of this soon, the hospital was going to be overflowing with casualties and I would only have myself to blame.

CHAPTER FOURTEEN

I AWOKE the next morning to an urgent text from Corinne, asking me to come to the house. Something must have happened with Rosalie. I changed as quickly as I could and sped across town, hopeful that Deputy Guthrie hadn't set any speed traps.

"The cause is supernatural," Adele said, the moment I arrived. "My bones don't lie."

"The cause of what?" I asked. "Did something else happen?"

"She's gone blind," Adele said. "Yesterday." The older witch's expression was tired and strained.

"We've tried several spells to help her regain her sight," Corinne added. "I raided the herb garden and even tried to come up with a mixture on my own. Nothing worked."

"I believe you," I said. "I'm just not sure what's responsible."

Angry heat radiated from Corinne. "Someone's cursed her obviously. We need to find the party responsible and make them reverse it."

"Where is she now?" I asked.

"Sleeping in the bedroom," Corinne said. "She doesn't seem to last more than two hours at a time though. She has to be exhausted."

Like the two of you, I wanted to say.

"Her behavior has been off in the days leading up to this," I said.

Adele gave me a sharp look. "And?"

"I don't think it's a coincidence."

"So whoever cursed her used some sort of escalating spell," Corinne said, as if that solved the matter. "This curse was designed to punish."

"Aren't most curses?" I asked. I still wasn't convinced a curse was to blame. Maybe if Rosalie's condition was an isolated incident, but it wasn't. First Hank's behavior escalated into a serious physical condition and now Rosalie. I felt confident that the two were connected, as well as the other behavioral issues that manifested this week.

"We need to find the responsible party," Adele said. "Someone is out to get my baby girl."

"This isn't a single supernatural's revenge," I said.

Adele lifted a finely plucked eyebrow. "Then what is it?"

If only I knew. I leaned my back against the countertop and addressed the two witches. "Walk me through Rosalie's week. Tell me everything you know."

Corinne and Adele glanced at each other with uncertainty. "Mom doesn't share everything. She likes to do her own thing."

"Fair enough." As far as I was concerned, my own mother revealed too many details about her schedule.

Adele tapped her fingernails on the countertop. "She had a date with a man called Farley earlier this week. As far as I know, it went well."

"Plus he's human," Corinne added. "He doesn't know about magic, let alone how to use it."

"I told Rosalie it was unfair to date an unsuspecting human," Adele continued, "but she said it was only a meaningless fling and not to worry."

"Any chance she was wrong about him?" I asked. Certain kinds of demons could disguise themselves as human, although that didn't explain the other affected residents.

Adele shook her head. "I took the liberty of researching him before the date." Her lips formed a thin smile. "Old habits die hard, it seems. Farley is a Twisse."

Ah. I recognized the name of one of the original Puritan families. Definitely human then.

"I don't know why she insists on wasting her time with humans when she knows the relationship can't go anywhere." Adele's gaze was drawn to a portrait on the wall across the room—a drawing of the three LeRoux witches. Corinne was probably six years old with untamed hair and a gap-toothed smile. "I like to think we're enough for each other, but I suppose that's unrealistic."

Corinne inched closer to hug her grandmother. "Let's not focus on that right now. The important thing is to figure out what happened to her so we can fix it."

"I don't think Farley Twisse is a concern, but I'm happy to check him out if it would make you feel better," I offered. At this point, I couldn't be too careful. I had no leads and more supernatural-induced issues than I could count.

Adele nodded gratefully. "Anything you can do, Eden."

"What else can you think of?" I prompted. "A new client? Did she mention anything unusual happening to her or around her this past week?"

"No new clients," Corinne said. "She read fortunes at a party for the Gunnars earlier in the week, but she's done work for them before. I'm pretty sure they know my mom's a fraud, but they eat it up all the same." She smiled to herself. "Mom does put on quite a performance."

"She did say she felt queasy afterward," Adele said.

Corinne shook her head dismissively. "That's only because the Gunnars hosted their party on a yacht this time. It was Mrs. Gunnar's sixtieth birthday and she wanted something special."

"A yacht?" I repeated.

"That's right," Corinne said. "They don't own it. They rented it from the marina. Mom doesn't do well on boats. The pay was too good to pass up, though, and she adores the Gunnars."

My brain was stuck on the boat. "Which day was this?"

Corinne pulled out her phone and checked the calendar. "Friday evening."

My breathing hitched. That was the same day that Father Kevin was on the water with the Mastersons.

"Was anyone else we know at the party?" I asked. If there was another known entity involved where we could establish baseline behavior, that might help me fit the pieces of the supernatural puzzle together. Right now, it seemed more like a Rorschach test.

Adele snapped her fingers. "Charity Grace."

Perfect. I knew all three Graces well enough to determine whether there was something amiss.

"Thanks," I said. "You've given me a lot to work with." I still wasn't sure how the Chesapeake Bay figured into any of this, but I had to keep digging.

"If you need any magical assistance," Corinne added, "you know where to find me."

Adele's gaze shifted to the closed bedroom door where Rosalie continued to sleep. "I know our families have had their differences, but I believe in you, Eden. I believe in what you're capable of and I know you'll do whatever you can to help Rosalie."

"I will, Adele. I promise."

. . .

Farley Twisse owned the miniature golf course that was located on the southern end of town. It was situated nicely with a view of the bay and a fudge shop and ice cream parlor on the next block, which his family also owned. The Twisse family had owned acres of waterfront land at one point and had sold parcels of it to developers over the years.

I didn't know Farley, but I recognized him immediately thanks to his resemblance to his father. They both had faded blond hair that looked stark white in the bright sunlight. They also shared the same 'dad bod' physique where the gut appeared slightly too large for the chosen trousers. Gilbert Twisse had been friends with Calybute Danforth, the owner of *The Buttermilk Bugle*, and I still remembered the two of them driving around town in Gilbert's convertible when I was a kid. I'd fallen in love with the Mustang and had begged each of my parents to buy one as the family vehicle. It was one of the few times I'd tried to use manipulation tactics based on their divorce. I'd overestimated the level of guilt they felt, apparently. Neither parent would even pretend to consider such an impractical car and my father ranted about the cost of filling the gas tank for a solid month. I was only eleven, but I became well-versed in cars after that attempt to persuade them. My father made sure that I understood that cars lost their value the minute you drove them off the lot and I was subjected to discussions about leasing versus owning. Anyone who leased a car, according to my father, failed the idiot test and deserved whatever punishments were handed out to them. It was also the beginning of his lessons on gas prices and oil checks. Ah, memories.

"Hello Farley," I said. I approached the counter where he stood in front of rows of clubs and different colored balls.

"Here to play?" he asked, his tone friendly. "How many will there be in your group?"

"I'd love to play," I lied. In truth, I couldn't handle mini-golf because I knew I'd want to win and that wasn't really within the spirit of the game. Last time I checked, mini-golf wasn't a competitive sport. "Unfortunately, I'm here for another reason."

His brow lifted. "Are you a lawyer? Because that kid wasn't looking where he was going. His mom told him to stay away from the edge of the volcano, but he didn't listen." His gaze drifted to the eleventh hole where a makeshift volcano flowed with pretend lava.

"I'm not a lawyer," I said. I flashed my badge. "My name is Agent Eden Fury. I'm here to ask a few questions about Rosalie LeRoux."

He recoiled. "FBI? I knew there was something phony about Rosalie. Is she involved in some kind of catfishing scheme?"

"No."

"Pyramid scheme?"

"No," I said.

He leaned forward. "Did she organize a fake festival and then disappear with the money?"

"No." I drummed my fingers on the counter. How was I going to phrase this to a human without saying too much? "Rosalie is experiencing some serious issues and we think it's due to a toxin she may have been exposed to within the last week. We know the two of you went out and I was hoping you could walk me through your time together."

Farley's features were etched with concern. "She's sick? Like she might die?"

"Right now she's blind," I said.

A gasp escaped him. "Are you sure?"

"Well, she can't see anything, so yeah."

He fiddled with a small yellow pencil on the counter. "What kind of toxin? Some secret government one?"

"No, nothing to do with us. We just know that exposure likely took place sometime between Friday and Wednesday and we'd like to narrow that down to help pinpoint the source."

Farley touched his throat. "Do I need to worry about exposure?" He forced a cough. "I have been feeling a little off this week."

"Can you describe your symptoms?"

"Itchy eyes and throat. Fatigue." He seemed to be trying to conjure up more plausible symptoms.

"Problems holding the remote?"

His eyes blazed with possibilities. "Yes, and I'm hungry all the time even though I don't feel well."

"Hmm. I think it's testosterflu," I said. Otherwise known as man flu, not that I'd tell him that.

"Should I see a doctor?"

"No, my sister-in-law is a doctor in town and she told me for a fact that what you have will clear up within twenty-four hours."

He appeared visibly relieved. "That's good news. But that's not what Rosalie has?"

"Sadly not."

Farley tapped the end of the pencil on the counter. "Rosalie and I didn't go anywhere special. I can't think of anything we did that would result in a...a toxin." He frowned. "Do bodily fluids count as toxins?"

I held up a hand. "No, Mr. Twisse. I think we're good."

He squinted at me. "Did you say your name was Fury?"

"That's right."

"Your family lives on Munster Close, on the old Wentworth farm."

And Alice Wentworth's ghost lives in the attic with me. That's right. "Yes, I'm in the process of having the barn converted into a small house."

"Cool," Farley said. "My grandfather used to talk about the Wentworths. He talked about a lot of the original families. He was in that club."

"What club is that?"

"Oh, I guess a Fury wouldn't know. The original Puritan families that settled Chipping Cheddar have a private club. It's been around for over a hundred years."

"How exclusive. Why aren't you a member?" I asked.

Farley shrugged. "Seemed kind of old-fashioned to me. My father didn't join either. He never liked all the secrecy. He preferred to be inclusive. It was better for business."

"Good for him," I said. It was hard enough growing up as a supernatural in a human town without worrying about the prominence of your family too. I vaguely remembered a pecking order of sorts, but I didn't pay much attention to it. The descendants of the original families seemed more interested in establishing a hierarchy, obviously because they pictured themselves at the top, not realizing that supernaturals could topple their regime with the sweep of a broomstick.

"Do you think I should check on Rosalie? I feel bad that I haven't texted. I've been busy."

I glanced around the nearly empty golf course. Farley and I seemed to have different ideas about what constituted busy.

"She can't read a text, so whatever you send will have to be read to her by someone else."

He shook his head in disbelief. "It's such a shock. I like Rosalie. She's a lot of fun. She even read my fortune earlier this week." He chuckled to himself. "Told me I'd soon meet a wonderful woman who'd sweep me off my feet."

I smiled. "And did she happen to describe this woman?"

"I'll put it this way—she has heaps of confidence. I like

that in a woman." He tugged his earlobe. "I sure hope she recovers."

"Is there anything unusual you remember about your time with her? Did you see anything out of the ordinary? Smell, taste? Anything at all?"

Farley contemplated the question. "Nothing comes to mind. I'm sorry. I wish I knew. It was all pretty nice and normal."

It struck me as odd to hear that anything associated with Rosalie LeRoux was 'nice and normal,' but Farley seemed genuine.

"Thanks for your time, Mr. Twisse. I appreciate it. If you think of anything, please call me." I scribbled my number on one of the tiny score sheets.

"If you ever feel like playing golf, come on by," he said. "I can also give you ten percent off on any fudge or ice cream." He motioned down the block. "My brother George manages the shops and I manage the golf course. Sometimes we swap, but I do my best to steer clear of the sweets." He patted his stomach. "My brother doesn't need to worry so much, but I inherited my dad's shape."

"Thanks for the offer. I'm sure I'll see you around," I said. As tempted as I was by the prospect of fudge and ice cream, I knew I had to save it for another time. Although I'd ruled out Farley Twisse, I was still no closer to figuring out what happened to Rosalie or anyone else—and if Hank and Rosalie's current conditions were any indication, things were about to take a turn for the worse.

CHAPTER FIFTEEN

I ARRIVED home from the mini-golf course and ran into the house to use the bathroom before I headed over to see Charity Grace. If Charity had attended the same party as Rosalie, maybe she was also experiencing issues.

When I emerged from the bathroom, I heard Aunt Thora's scratchy voice singing *You Sexy Thing*. I found her in the kitchen holding a broomstick like a microphone. She waved to me and carried on singing. I noticed Olivia on the sofa wearing oversized headphones. She pulled one side away from her ear when she spotted me.

"Aunt Eden, she won't stop making noise."

Aunt Thora popped a lemon on the handle of the broomstick to make a head and danced around the island with it. I could see why she and Ted got along so well.

"She's in a good mood," I said. "Why rain on her parade?"

"Why not? She rained on mine. She told me I should be reading at a higher level," Olivia complained.

I shot a quizzical glance at Aunt Thora. That sounded like the sort of thing Grandma would say.

Aunt Thora shrugged. "We have to encourage her if we

expect her to reach for the stars. We didn't have to do that with you, of course. You were chomping at the bit to achieve right out of the womb."

Olivia ripped off her headphones and tossed them onto the cushion. "It isn't nice to compare. I'm my own person." She grabbed a coloring book and a box of crayons from the end table. "I don't know who let Ryan color in this book. He can't stay in the lines like I can. That boy is impossible."

"He's a year old, Olivia," I said. "We're lucky he's coloring with the crayon and not eating it."

Aunt Thora started to use the broom to sweep the kitchen floor, breathing in the scent of the lemon while she worked. "Anton used to eat crayons. For a few months, your mother worried that he was going to be a garbage demon."

"There's a garbage demon?" Olivia asked. "Is that what Oscar the Grouch is?"

"Quite possibly," Aunt Thora said.

"Why have I never heard this story?" I asked.

Aunt Thora flicked the broom. "Oh, you know your mother. She likes to sweep things under the rug. Kind of like I'm doing now. Ha!" She smiled at me.

"Since when does my mom like to hide anything?" I countered. "She's all about flaunting it in your face."

"She can be discreet," Aunt Thora said. "She hexed that awful Tanner Hughes to save you from a lifetime of misery with that narcissist. She didn't flaunt that, did she?"

I stopped and turned around slowly to face her. "I'm sorry. When did she hex Tanner?" I was certain I'd remember that.

Aunt Thora set the broom against the wall. "When you were in high school. She wanted to make sure you didn't hitch your wagon to a human, so she fixed it."

"Define 'fixed.'" My tone was sharper than I intended. Olivia must've sensed the tension because she jumped off the sofa and fled to the guest bedroom where she often stayed overnight.

Aunt Thora seemed incapable of keeping anything to herself right now. Surprisingly, she didn't even try to lie. "She hexed Tanner so that he slept with Sassafras Persimmons. She knew Sassafras had a thing for the boy, so your mother saw it as a way to extricate you from the relationship. You know she never approved of dating humans."

Every vein in my body pushed against the surface of my skin, ready to burst. "How long have you known about this?"

Aunt Thora appeared entirely nonchalant, despite the bombshell she was dropping. "Since it happened. Esther helped her, of course. Those two are always in cahoots."

My hands moved to my hips. "And you?"

"I was too busy with my own family then to get involved," Aunt Thora said. "I thought it was a terrible idea. You know I always resented them for talking me out of a relationship with Ted O'Neill back in the day."

All that heartbreak. All that misery. Feelings of not being good enough. Pretty enough. Blonde enough. They were all based on a lie. A hex. The kitchen swayed and I leaned against the island for support.

"I'm surprised you never figured it out." Aunt Thora continued babbling, seemingly oblivious to the emotional crisis I was on the verge of having. My world had tilted on its axis and my head was too busy spinning.

"Aunt Eden?" Olivia appeared in the kitchen, clutching a zombie doll she called Carol. "Are you upset?"

I fought for breath. "No, I'm fine," I lied. "I stubbed my toe."

Olivia cocked her head. "It's okay to be upset. You don't have to hide it. Mommy always says that emotions are how we express what we're feeling and we shouldn't be ashamed of them."

Aunt Thora and I gaped at the little girl.

"Well, you didn't learn it from your daddy, that's for sure," Aunt Thora said.

"Thank the gods for Verity," I added. "Listen, it's grown-up stuff. Aunt Thora told me something I didn't know and it was upsetting news, even though it happened a long time ago."

"Did someone die?" Olivia asked.

"Nothing like that," I said.

Olivia shoved the doll at me. "Zombies make everything better." She made the doll kiss me and its head immediately popped off. Somehow that seemed appropriate.

"Thanks, Olivia," I said.

She managed to snatch the head off the floor before Charlemagne swallowed it. "Aunt Thora, you've been acting weird. You don't usually talk this much. Mommy always says you're like a polite ghost."

"No, that would be Alice," I said. I shifted my focus to my great-aunt. "Have you upped your caffeine intake?" Olivia was right. Aunt Thora seemed more energetic than usual. Now that I thought about it, she'd been chattier than usual all week. I'd been so focused on people like Father Kevin that it hadn't registered. I realized that even my mother's unusual issue was likely tied to whatever the supernatural occurrence was.

"No change in my diet," Aunt Thora said.

Before I could ask anything else, I heard the front door open and my mother's laughter drifted into the kitchen. I couldn't handle seeing her right now. I had too much on my plate to waste time on anger and resentment. That confrontation would have to wait.

I glanced at Aunt Thora. "You're going to tell her I know, aren't you?"

"Don't think I could stop myself if I wanted to," came the honest reply. "I have verbal diarrhea."

I bent over and kissed Olivia's head before slipping out the back door to avoid my mother. I walked to the front of the house and continued along the sidewalk until I reached the Graces' house. There was no answer at the front door so I ventured to their backyard oasis. Aggie sat in an Adirondack chair wearing a wide brimmed sunhat and dark sunglasses. She looked like an aging Audrey Hepburn.

"Aggie?"

"Afternoon, Eden. I'm resting my eyes. Why don't you have a seat?"

My pulse sped up. "You're not blind, are you?"

She laughed softly. "Blind? No, dear." She removed the glasses to show me the sliced cucumber on either closed eyelid. "See? Resting." She removed the cucumber slices and peered at me. "What's the matter?"

"You can tell, huh?"

She smiled sympathetically. "With you? I can always tell. I still remember you barging in here as a little girl with tales of woe. Your expression always gave you away."

"I used to come here to vent about my family, so I guess that doesn't surprise me."

"You and your brother used to fight like vampires and werewolves," she said. "It's wonderful that you've been able to overcome your differences. I don't know what I'd do without my sisters."

"Speaking of sisters..." I swiveled my head to see if Charity or Thalia was within view. "How are they?"

Aggie angled her hat to keep out the shifting sunlight. "Why do I sense an agenda in that simple question?"

I exhaled. "Adele mentioned at the supernatural council meeting that Rosalie was out of sorts."

"Rosalie LeRoux is always out of sorts."

"Yes, well. Now she's blind."

Aggie stiffened. "Blind? Whatever happened?"

"That's what I'm trying to figure out. There's been a spate of uncharacteristic behavior this week—Rosalie included. Then one affected man suffered a heart attack and nearly drowned. Rosalie's blind." I hesitated. "You can see where this is going."

Aggie instinctively glanced toward the house. "Like the chaos demon."

"Sort of. Maybe." It wasn't a chaos demon this time though. The circumstances were too different and that demon was long gone. "You're hiding something."

Aggie bit her lip. "My sister. She hasn't been herself for the past few days and she can't seem to shake it."

"In what way?"

"It started as a creative block. You know how she's always sculpting or painting." Aggie motioned to a blank canvas on the opposite side of the garden. "She set that out days ago, hoping for inspiration to strike."

"Obviously nothing did."

Aggie shook her head. "She's so depressed that she's taken to her room and only comes out for meals."

"At least she's still eating."

"I don't know for how long," Aggie said. "If she's suffering like the others, then this could be very bad indeed."

"Why haven't you said anything?" I asked.

"I thought she was in a funk," Aggie said. "It happens every few decades or so. A long life can have that effect."

I thought of my own immortality. "Does it ever happen to you?"

"Ennui? Naturally, dear. When you live in this world long enough, it's inevitable. Watch loved ones pass on and leave you behind. It's not the dream many believe it to be." She seemed to remember the recent addition to my fury traits. "I'm so sorry, Eden. I didn't mean..."

"It's okay," I said. "I've been interested in the topic for obvious reasons."

Aggie's pale cheeks burned pink. "I do apologize, Eden. It was a thoughtless remark. There are so many wonderful reasons to embrace your immortality."

"The most important one being that I can't do anything to change it," I said ruefully. "Honestly, though, I'm not here about that right now. My priority is whatever's happening to residents like your sister and Rosalie." Whatever it was, it was impacting humans and supernaturals alike.

Aggie struggled to her feet. "Would you like a drink? I have a lovely herbal tea that Thalia made from the garden."

"No thanks. Would it be okay if I speak to Charity?" I asked. "I promise I won't ask too many questions."

"She's very lethargic, as you can imagine," Aggie said. "But I'll do anything to help her."

I followed Aggie into the house, through the kitchen, and up a back staircase. She knocked gently on the first door on the left and a tired voice responded.

"Aggie?" she croaked.

"Yes, it's me. I'm here with Eden Fury. She'd like to speak to you about an important matter."

"Yes, of course." The reply was clearer, as though she were making an extra effort to seem normal.

Aggie pushed open the door and I entered, completely encompassed by darkness. The shades were drawn and there was no light in the room.

"I'm sorry to bother you," I said. "I'm investigating a situation for the FBM and I think you might be...involved." I resisted the impulse to say 'a victim' and make her feel worse than she already did.

Charity's eyelids fluttered. "Involved?" she asked softly. "You think I've inadvertently left a magic trail or something?"

"No, no," I said. "I don't mean that you're responsible." I perched on the edge of an antique chair next to the bedside table. "I think your current condition is a result of supernatural activity and I'm trying to pinpoint the cause."

Charity's relief was palpable. "I thought it was depression. It happens every now and again, although not very often. I just couldn't decide whether my creativity was blocked because of depression or the other way around."

I reached over and squeezed her arm. "I don't think it's either one. I think you've been influenced by an external force."

Charity lifted her head off the pillow. "Depression is very much like a demon sitting on your chest. Are you sure?"

"Others have been impacted differently," I said. "I'm trying to understand the connections and locate the source. I understand you were on the Chesapeake this past weekend for a party."

"Yes, the Gunnars. You think it might be something in the water?"

"Not necessarily, but several of those affected were on or near the water earlier this week." That didn't explain Clara or Aunt Thora, though. To my knowledge, neither of them had been on the water or at the marina recently. At the thought of Clara, my chest tightened. Clara had ended our friendship so abruptly. I couldn't bear the thought of anything happening to her before I could fix it.

"There was nothing strange about the party," Charity said. "Everyone seemed normal and I didn't sense anything amiss."

"What about Rosalie LeRoux?"

Charity coughed. "She's always amiss."

I couldn't argue with that assessment. "Can you think of

anything out of the ordinary that you encountered this week, before your creativity stalled?"

Charity propped herself up by resting her cheek in the palm of her hand. "Nothing unusual. This week was my typical routine. Advised a few clients. Met a friend for lunch in town."

"What about the rest of the weekend?"

Charity's eyes rolled upward as she pondered the question. "I went out to dinner with a friend. We went to a few bars afterward. She's single and looking to mingle." A faint smile passed her lips.

"You're single," I pointed out. "You didn't want to mingle?"

Charity flopped back onto the pillow. "I'd much rather sculpt or paint. Geriatric men don't really do it for me."

"No wizards or warlocks?" I asked. "No magic users that may have targeted you?"

Charity squirmed under the sheet. "No. Just rowdy humans. Svetlana talked to a couple of them, but I stayed at the table. They'd had too much to drink to be worthy of conversation. Then again, nothing seems worthy of anything to me these days."

"Thanks for your help, Charity. I hope you get your hands dirty in the clay again soon."

The Grace sister stared blankly at the ceiling, her eyes brimming with unshed tears. "Me too, Eden."

CHAPTER SIXTEEN

NEVILLE and I were in the middle of drafting a list of all the people and supernaturals that seemed impacted and what their behavioral changes were when an impatient knock at the door interrupted us.

"Add the name Gloria to the list," I said, walking to answer the door.

"Wait. What if it's a Jehovah's Witness?" Neville asked.

"Why would it be a Jehovah's Witness? This is an office."

"Bring a piece of candy," Neville called.

I turned to stare at him. "They're not trick-or-treating. And if anyone's trying to convert me, I'll show them my crown of snakes. Problem solved." I flung open the door to see Sassy. Given what I'd recently learned about Tanner, Sassy wasn't on the list of people I wanted to see right now.

"I have to talk to you about Clara," Sassy said. She brushed past me and barged straight into the office.

Neville shot me an anxious look, but I ignored him. I couldn't get rid of Sassy easily without raising suspicion.

"Unfortunately, Clara and I aren't on speaking terms at the moment," I said.

"I know, and now neither are we," Sassy said. "She said awful things about Tanner and I just couldn't listen to another word. She sounded so heartless. It's not like her." Sassy seemed to notice the office for the first time. "Pretty shabby for the FBI. I guess this is what a government budget can afford."

I returned to the computer. "As it happens, Neville and I are in the midst of an assignment right now. I'd be happy to commiserate about Clara later…"

"And here I thought you were the one knocked out of alignment," Sassy continued, ignoring my polite hint. "I think you both need to come to Francine's special yoga class and sort yourselves out. Between her fourth chakra and your…" She gave me the once-over. "All your chakras, you could both use it. A few low lunges for Clara and a complete body transplant for you and we can all be friends again."

"I have no clue what you're talking about," I said. "I thought you said my spine was out of alignment."

"Well, I'm sure that's true based on your posture, but I was referring to chakras."

"Chakras?" I repeated. The things they talked about in yoga class that made my eyes glaze over whenever they were mentioned?

Sassy rolled her eyes. "The energy centers in our bodies that control our qualities. If the chakras aren't balanced, then our inner self can't be at peace. Do you just take naps with your eyes open during yoga or what?"

"Sassy, thank you so much for stopping by and expressing your concern," I said. I practically pushed her out the door.

"Then you'll come to Advanced Inner Peace?" Sassy asked. "I'll make sure Clara shows up too, even if I have to strap her to my back. I mean, she's being cruel, but she's still my friend, you know? I haven't had many good girlfriends—or any…" She trailed off.

I got her as far as the door, when guilty feet ground me to a halt. "When's the class?"

"I think it's Friday afternoon, but I'll text you for sure."

"I would appreciate that." I paused. "You're not going to lose Clara, okay? Her issue..."

"Fourth chakra."

"Her fourth chakra is going to be aligned again before you know it."

She beamed. "Yes, that's what Advanced Inner Peace is for." She slipped out the door and I locked it behind her.

"You're not actually going to attempt advanced yoga, are you?" Neville asked.

I hurried back to the computer. "Weren't you listening?"

"Not closely," he admitted. "I tend to get distracted by the rest of her."

I groaned. "Typical man." I ran a quick internet search on chakras and compared the information with the list we'd created. "I think Sassy is onto something."

"Sorry, what?" Neville blinked in confusion.

"Come and see," I said. "Father Kevin lost his faith. That's the crown chakra. His connection to the divine spirit. Soul energy. My mother is having sex-related issues. That's her sacral chakra, the second one."

Neville peered over my shoulder. "John Maclaren and Charity Grace have blocked creativity and depression. Those are also the sacral chakra."

"Aunt Thora can't stop talking," I said, which included revealing secrets. Thank the gods she didn't know mine. "That's her throat chakra."

"What about Rosalie?" Neville asked.

"Her third eye chakra," I said. I thought of Verity's uptick in seemingly unrelated ailments. Migraines, digestive issues, arthritis, nerve pain—they were all attributable to imbalanced chakras. It only took a few minutes to connect each affected party on the list to a corresponding chakra.

"Okay, so what does it mean when everybody's chakras have been knocked out of alignment around the same time?" I asked.

"Perhaps someone has cast a spell," Neville suggested. "It would take an awful lot of magic to influence so many in town though. Who's that powerful, aside from your family?"

"A spell? But why would someone want our chakras imbalanced? A yoga studio owner desperate for business? Seems far-fetched."

"We're talking about the supernatural realm, Agent Fury. Everything is far-fetched."

True enough. I typed 'chakras' in the search bar of the FBM database. Fifteen hundred results? Yikes.

"You'll need to narrow that down," Neville said.

"You think?"

He leaned beside me. "May I?"

I shifted over so he could use the keyboard. He added 'imbalance' and 'confluence.'

"Ooh, confluence," I said. "There's a fancy word."

"And useful as well." He tapped the screen. The results had been narrowed to thirty. "I'll take the first fifteen, shall I?"

"Sounds good to me." If Clara's heart chakra truly was out of alignment, then she was at risk for a heart attack like Hank. His heart chakra was also the one imbalanced, but in the opposite direction. I had to help her before it was too late.

Neville hit print and took his page to his own desk to continue the research.

"I never wanted to work behind a desk, yet here I am," I said. Clicking and reading and printing. "I might as well have been a lawyer or something equally boring."

"Equally boring?" Neville echoed. "Agent Fury, you catch demons for a living. You harness magic powers for a living. How can that possibly compare with the law?"

"I miss the FBI, Neville. I'm sorry, but I do." That job had been my dream and I'd achieved it, only to have it taken away because of my stupid fury powers.

"I'm not offended," Neville said. "I know it isn't personal."

I turned to look at him. "Good, because it really isn't. I liked working in the field. I liked working with Fergus." Although he probably didn't like working with me after I bit him, not that he remembered. "I liked being far away from my family."

"If you'd stayed in San Francisco, you would never have met Chief Fox."

"Good point." And one that I couldn't dismiss. I'd never met anyone like Sawyer Fox. The idea of not meeting him—it wasn't one I wanted to ponder.

I scanned number nineteen on the list of results. "What about a sorceress that specializes in sexuality?"

"Like a magic prostitute?"

I swiveled my chair to face him. "Are we even researching the same subject? No, not a magic hooker. A sorceress who messes with people's sexuality for the fun of it."

Neville considered the idea. "I would say it had potential, except it isn't simply sexuality that's been affected."

"No, that's true," I said. "It's too narrow." I turned back to the computer and continued to read. "We're definitely looking for something broader in scope than a magic hooker."

"Seriously, though, aren't all hookers magical?" Neville cleared his throat. "That was a joke."

"I figured." I moved on to the next one on the list and my heart skipped a beat.

"Here's one involving a grief demon," Neville said. "Depression could explain a lot of what's happened."

"This is it," I said. I barely registered his suggestion. "There's an actual chakra demon." And it was literally called a chakra demon. So much for prioritizing search results.

"I suppose it isn't like the Santa Claus of chakras," Neville said. "Doesn't sneak down your chimney and deliver you pools of energy."

"Not quite." I read slowly, trying to absorb the details.

Neville came back to read over my shoulder. "Oh, dearie me. It certainly does sound like the culprit, doesn't it?"

"The chakra demon's main goal is to knock chakras out of alignment, leaving chaos in its wake," I read aloud. "It will tap into a person's previously balanced chakra and send it spinning on its axis."

"It seems we have a chakra demon on the loose in Chipping Cheddar," Neville said. "I'll check the reports to see if anyone has reported one missing from Otherworld."

I kept reading while he checked the reams of paper that had come through this week.

"I think I found a possibility," he said. "A chakra demon was reported wreaking havoc in Mexico. Agents there lost track of it and there's been no activity since then."

"Probably hiding on a beach in a bottle of tequila. That's what I'd do." I stopped. "Wait, did you say Mexico?"

Neville reread the report. "Altamira, a port city."

I smacked my forehead. "You've got to be kidding me. The demon hitched a ride here on a party bus."

"And it's been enjoying quite the party since its arrival," Neville said.

"That explains why it started with people on the water," I said. "The party bus arrived by boat on Friday. The demon infected people like Father Kevin and Jarvis first and then more people became unbalanced as the party bus made its way around town."

"Does it have to touch the person?" Neville asked. He scanned the information. "Ah, I see. It's in the haze category."

"Like the chaos demon?" It took the form of fog that had spread across the town.

"Not quite but a similar effect," Neville said.

"Is it solid enough that we can apprehend it?"

"There's always a way to apprehend it," Neville said.

I leaned my elbows on the desk. "How will we find it? There've been no reports of unusual sightings in the supernatural community." And humans wouldn't be able to see it anyway.

Neville tapped a paragraph on the screen. "What are demons always drawn to?"

"Power," I said. "You think we should check the portal and the vortex?"

"It's a good start. We shouldn't pursue the demon until we have a plan ready to exact at a moment's notice," Neville said.

"I totally agree."

We stared at each other for a moment. Neither one of us knew where to start.

"There's nothing in the records about stopping them?" I asked.

"Not that I saw," Neville said. "They happen to be rare demons."

Naturally. Why should wrangling a chakra demon be easy?

"Shouldn't there be a Dummies' Guide to Demons or something?" I asked. I'd even take the CliffsNotes version at this point.

"I could ask in the wizard forum..." Neville began.

"No, we shouldn't need to ask for outside help," I said.

"There has to be more information available. If we search hard enough, we'll find it."

"Excellent point, Agent Fury," Neville said. "I excelled in research. I have no doubt I can uncover the information we need."

He managed it in less than an hour thanks to a call to the FBM's Mexican headquarters.

"I didn't know you spoke Spanish, Neville," I said.

"I don't," he said. "I used a translator spell."

I gaped at him. "There's still so much I don't know."

The wizard smiled proudly. "I'm glad you said that and not me."

"How do we stop it?" I asked.

"We need seven crystals, one for each chakra," Neville said.

"Any seven crystals?"

The wizard snorted. "When have you known things to be that easy, Agent Fury?"

I resisted the urge to sulk. "Let me guess. Seven incredibly rare crystals."

"Yes. Each one corresponds to a chakra. I have four of them here as part of the FBM's collection," he said.

"Four chakra crystals?" That seemed odd.

"No, the crystals aren't only designed for catching a chakra demon. They're used for all sorts of magic. The rarer ones obviously fuel the most powerful spells so we try to keep a small supply."

"Which crystals do we have?"

"The ones for the throat, sacral, heart, and navel. We still need three though."

"Which three?" I went to read his handwritten notes. "Red beryl for the root chakra, benitoite for the third eye, and taaffeite for the crown."

"I could put in a request from headquarters, but that will take time," Neville said.

"We don't have the luxury," I said. I went back to my desk to retrieve my purse.

"Where are you going?"

"We need rare crystals," I said. "I happen to know a guy who knows a guy."

Neville arched an eyebrow. "Care to elaborate?"

I heaved a sigh. "Uncle Moyer. He's got black market contacts. I bet he can source what we need faster than the FBM."

"You're proposing to use illegal means on behalf of a federal agency?" he asked, incredulous.

"Neville, would you exceed the speed limit for the sake of an emergency mission?"

The wizard tapped his cheek thoughtfully. "I suppose it would depend…"

"No, Neville. It wouldn't depend. If it meant the difference between doing the job and not doing the job, you'd speed."

He hesitated. "Am I driving past a school? Is school in session?"

I groaned. "Just admit that you'd speed so I can make my point and get out of here."

Neville held up his chubby hands. "Yes. I would undoubtedly speed."

I bowed with a flourish. "Thank you."

CHAPTER SEVENTEEN

I DIDN'T BOTHER to call before showing up at Uncle Moyer's office, so I shouldn't have been surprised that he was busy with a client. I waited in the reception area, chatting with Connie, his assistant. Connie was like Clara, a human with the Sight. She was perfect for Uncle Moyer's business because her presence put the human clients at ease. Nobody came to Moyer the Lawyer unless they were desperate. The cost was generally too high and didn't always involve money.

I liked Connie. She and I often traded stories about our nieces and nephews. Hers were older than Olivia and Ryan, but not so old that she'd forgotten what they were like at the same ages.

"Gavin is all about Fortnite right now," Connie said. "You'd better hope something else comes along by the time they reach nine or ten. These games suck away their souls."

"I would think you'd approve of that," I said, with a nod toward the closed office door. Uncle Moyer was well known for trading favors for souls. The right soul fetched an excellent price in the underworld.

Connie smirked and continued to file her nails at the desk. My mother would've hexed her for that.

"I'm here for a paycheck, not to pass judgment," Connie said. "Besides, Moyer is a good boss."

"Then it's a mutual admiration society. Uncle Moyer says you're the best secretary he's ever had."

"Why do you call him your uncle anyways?" Connie asked. "I've always wanted to ask."

"Anton started it when we were kids," I said. "Because he was Aunt Thora's son, we thought everybody in her immediate family was an aunt or an uncle. The title stuck."

Connie's nose wrinkled. "Cute."

The office door opened and a man in a cheap polyester suit emerged, wiping the sweat from his brow. It had either been a tough negotiation or this guy had dodged a bullet.

"Do you need to make another appointment, Mr. Hedley?" Connie asked sweetly.

"No thank you," he said. He ducked his head and left the office, avoiding eye contact with me.

"Moyer, your cousin Eden is here," Connie called over her shoulder. She moved on to the nails on the other hand.

"What an unexpected surprise," he said. "Come in, gorgeous."

I entered his office and closed the door behind me in case his next client was early. I sat across from him and immediately began to play with the Darth Vader bobblehead on the edge of the desk.

"Mr. Hedley looked a little unsure about whatever arrangement he made with you."

Uncle Moyer wore a vague smile. "He wants a trophy wife and he seems willing to part with quite a bit to make that happen."

"Based on that cheap suit, I'm guessing it's not a hefty bank account he'll be parting with."

"That's confidential, Eden. You know that."

"Does he at least get to choose the trophy wife?"

"That will be a separate negotiation with her," Uncle Moyer said. "As it happens, I already have someone in mind."

"Lawyer turned matchmaker, huh?"

"I serve my clients as best I can." He smacked my hand away from the Darth Vader. "Now what brings you here?"

"Official business," I said. "I need someone with access to a private stock of rare crystals."

Uncle Moyer slotted his fingers together and leaned forward with enthusiasm. "Go on."

"I have to stop a chakra demon and I need three rare crystals to do it."

Uncle Moyer sucked the air into his cheeks. "A chakra demon? I've never even heard of that one."

"It's apparently as rare as the crystals I need to capture it. Neville and I already have the other four." I named the three crystals I still needed.

"And what is the FBM prepared to offer in return?"

"To not arrest you for known violations of supernatural law," I said, directly meeting his gaze.

His jaw clenched. "Are you threatening me, dear cousin?"

"Not at all. I'm telling you the price, just as you asked."

His pursed lips melted into a smile. "Very shrewd. I'm so proud of you, I could burst."

"Please don't tell anyone," I said, shifting uncomfortably. "I don't like playing hardball with family."

"And yet you excel." He lifted his phone. "I have a few favors I can call in. How quickly do you need them?"

"Now," I said. "I have to catch this demon before anyone else gets hurt."

His dark eyes glimmered with understanding. "I think I know who I can call for one-stop shopping. He owes me big for keeping his family out of the underworld. I've been sitting on that particular IOU, but I believe now is an excellent time to call in repayment."

"Thanks."

He spun around in his chair and spoke in low tones to his contact. After a few exchanges, he hung up and turned to face me. "All sorted."

"Really?"

Uncle Moyer nodded. "They should be here momentarily."

The air over his desk began to shimmer and, one by one, three crystals dropped onto the desk—red, then blue, then a pinky purple.

"That's what I call direct mail," I said.

"He's a warlock," Uncle Moyer said.

"With deep pockets presumably."

"And even deeper mines." He motioned to the crystals. "They're all yours, dear cousin."

I scooped them into my hand. "I have a question—did you know my mother used magic to make Tanner cheat on me back in high school?"

He didn't need to answer. I could tell from the subtle lift of his brow that the news came as a surprise. "How did you find out?"

"Your mother, actually. Her throat chakra is out of alignment so she's spilling all the family secrets. If there's anything you want her to keep in the vault, you'd better hope I get to the demon before she can post it online." I stood to leave.

Uncle Moyer looked at me with concern. "Tell me, is this demon something Tomas and I should be worried about? Are we at risk too?"

I shook the crystals in my hand like I was about to roll a pair of lucky dice. "Not anymore."

. . .

With the crystals safely stowed in Neville's tiny bottomless bag, he and I wasted no time checking the powerful places in town like the portal and the vortex. Unfortunately, there was no sign of the chakra demon.

"I think it's because there's no one here," I said, standing on the vortex. "Power in a vacuum serves no purpose for this demon. The chakra demon thrives on throwing alignment out of whack. If there are no people or supers here, then there's nothing for the demon to do."

"Then it will most likely be searching for a concentration of chakras and power," Neville said.

"I'm sure that's its preference." I sighed. "At least we won't be having another supernatural council meeting this week. That would be sure to draw its attention." And none of us on the council had been affected yet.

"What about your house?" Neville asked. "There's certainly a concentration of power on Munster Close, especially on the Wentworth property."

"I don't know," I said. "My mother and Aunt Thora have already been whacked. It's not clear from the intel whether the demon would sense that and move on to someone else."

"I'll go back to the office and see what I can find out," Neville said. "Our Mexican counterparts were very helpful."

"Fine, I'll go home." I dreaded spending time there knowing that I wasn't ready to confront my mother.

Neville patted my arm. "It will all come out right in the end, Agent Fury. It always does."

"Except for the one time it doesn't." I thought of Paul Pidcock. The former agent probably would've laughed if someone had told him he'd die from bee stings generated by a fear demon.

I left the vortex and went home to make sure there was no chakra demon lurking in the shadows. My family was assembled in the kitchen when I arrived home.

"There you are," Grandma said, giving me a disapproving look. "Your poor hellhound has been desperate for a walk."

"Couldn't you walk her?" I asked. "It's not like you're busy."

"I'm not the one who decided to rescue her from the bowels of the underworld," Grandma said. "She's your responsibility."

The back door opened and my mother entered, holding the end of Princess Buttercup's leash. "This hound's legs are too long," she complained. "I was practically dragged down the close."

"You walked Princess Buttercup?" I asked in disbelief.

"I decided to exercise. I thought it might help ease my pent-up feelings."

"I thought you had a date, Beatrice," Aunt Thora said from her place in front of the stovetop.

"I cancelled," my mother said. "There's no point until this ridiculous phase passes."

Part of me wanted to stay silent on the subject, but I couldn't help myself. Despite what she did to me, I didn't want my mother to suffer. "As much as I hate to say this, your…libido will be back in action soon," I said.

My mother unleashed the hound and focused on me. "How do you know?"

"It's not you." I hesitated. "Well, it is you, but there's a demon responsible. It's called a chakra demon and it's messing with energy pools, including yours."

My mother yanked up her sleeves. "Where is it? I'll turn that piece of garbage into ash. Save you the trouble of paperwork."

I rolled my eyes. "A dead demon would only create more paperwork."

"Oh, well. You are oddly fond of paperwork. Where can I find it?" The murderous look in her eye gave me pause. The penalty for ruining her sex drive was apparently death. Surprising that Anton and I made it to adulthood.

"I'm handling this," I said. "It's official FBM business." I shouldn't have opened my big mouth, but I wanted to—what? Comfort her by letting her know that she would recover her mojo? What was wrong with me? Stupid perfectly aligned chakras.

"How are you handling it?" my mother asked. "How do you kill it?"

"I'm not going to kill it," I said. "I'm going to capture it and call the extraction team."

My mother tipped her head back and released a frustrated groan. "Such a do-gooder. Just kill it and tell them you tried to capture it, but it refused to cooperate. Problem solved."

"Yes, lying to the Federal Bureau of Magic sounds like a marvelous plan," I said.

"If you don't kill it, how will the chakras revert to their normal states?" Aunt Thora asked.

"According to our research, once it's out of range, the effects will diminish," I said. "The demon's been hanging around town, spreading its influence. The longer it stays, the worse the impact, which is why Rosalie went from demented to blind."

"Blind?" my mother asked softly.

"Yes, trust me. You've gotten off easy."

"No, I haven't," my mother said. "That's part of the problem."

I ignored her remark. "I just need to figure out where the demon will pop up next so I can trap it."

"Well, make sure you take care of it before Myrtle's funeral," Grandma said. "I don't need some animated corpse leaping out of the casket." She smiled to herself. "On second thought, that would liven things up a bit. So many stodgy witches in one place is a recipe for a coma. Maybe I'll bring my flask."

"It's not a necromancer," I said. "It's a chakra demon. Nothing will happen to Myrtle, but all the witches in one place..." Oh.

My mother looked at me sideways. "What?"

"That's where the chakra demon will show up next," I said. "All that power in one place. All that emotional energy. It's going to be too much to resist."

"I don't know about that," my mother said. "The only ones with any real power are the ones you already live with, sweetheart."

No. There would be the LeRoux witches, too, as well as a bevy of other supernaturals. A supernatural funeral would be like X marks the spot.

"I need to go," I said.

"You just got home," Aunt Thora objected. "You should at least sit and have a cup of tea. Your mother already complains that you don't spend enough time here."

"Aunt Thora!" my mother scolded her.

"Can't stay," I said, and turned on my heel abruptly. Right now my mother's complaints were the least of my concerns.

"Where are you going?" my mother called after me.

"Shopping. Apparently I need a tasteful black dress," I said. "Looks like I'm going to a funeral."

CHAPTER EIGHTEEN

I RODE in the backseat of my mother's car to Davenport Park. Grandma rode shotgun and Aunt Thora was in the back with me. It was only when we parked at Manchego Place that I realized where we were headed.

"Wait. Myrtle's funeral is being held on the vortex?"

"Of course," my mother said. "Where else?"

Now I knew with certainty the chakra demon would make an appearance here. I just had to stay alert and be ready to pounce.

We trudged up the hill to where two rows of chairs circled a casket. All the seats with a view of the Chesapeake had already been taken, so we had to settle for chairs in the second circle facing the river.

"I need to be on the end," Grandma said.

"It's a circle," I said. "There is no end."

"Tell that to my bladder. I need to be able to make a quick escape."

"And go where?" I demanded. "The nearest bathroom is the public toilet in the park."

With a huff of indignation, Grandma sat next to Aunt Thora.

"I can't believe she's in a casket," someone said in a stage whisper. "That's not our way."

"It's made from sustainable materials," her companion replied. "There's a funeral specialist that understands the needs of supernaturals."

"It would be better if it was just her body," the other woman said. "I don't care for these modern services."

My phone buzzed and I read a text from Neville letting me know that he'd arrived. I sent him a thumbs up emoji in response and put away my phone.

A witch across the circle began to cry so hard that she gasped for air. The wizard beside her handed her a handkerchief.

"I thought witches were more reserved," I whispered.

Grandma silenced me with a look. "It's a funeral. What do you expect? Everyone is busy contemplating their own mortality." She narrowed her eyes. "Except you—you immortal wench with your flaming eyeballs." She returned her attention to her phone screen where the Little Critters app was open.

"Grandma," I scolded her. "This is a funeral. Can't you stop the game for half an hour?"

"There's a critter here I need to catch. I've been trying to get this sucker for two weeks. If I don't catch him now, who knows how long it will be?"

"Show some respect for Myrtle," I said. "How would you feel if she played a game throughout your service?"

Grandma continued to play. "I'd be dead, so what would I care?"

My mother leaned over and whispered, "Funerals can bring out odd behavior. People feel vulnerable. Afraid even. I mean, any one of us can be next."

"It's not an Agatha Christie novel," Grandma shot back.

"It's sweet that your little friend decided to join you," my mother said. She wiggled a finger at Neville across the circle. "He follows you around like a lovesick puppy."

"He's not my little friend and he isn't lovesick. He's my assistant and we're here to stop a demon, remember?"

My mother reached across to pat my hand. "That's what they all say, sweetheart."

I brushed off her comment. I refused to take the bait, especially in the middle of a funeral *and* a mission.

Grandma hissed under her breath when she spotted Adele and Corinne slide into seats not far from Neville.

"You should be happy there are so many mourners here for Myrtle," I said.

"Oh, please. They're just here to see whether she makes good on her promise to haunt us for the rest of our lives."

I reeled back. "Myrtle said that?"

Grandma shrugged. "She might have had a little too much sherry that night. She also said she was going to ride through town on an elephant in nothing but her birthday suit."

I clucked my tongue. "And you said she was boring."

"Not drunk Myrtle. Drunk Myrtle was a hoot."

Before the service could begin, a gust of wind blew through the circle and I felt the energy shift. The hairs stood on the back of my neck. Showtime.

I took out my phone and sent a text to Neville. While everyone was busy mourning and gossiping, Neville had placed runes around the outside of the circle to keep the demon contained when it finally arrived—which it had.

An elderly witch stood to say a few words about Myrtle.

"Sit down," I yelled.

"Eden don't be rude," my mother said.

A shimmering haze appeared in the middle of the circle next to the casket. It reminded me of the bands of color produced by an oil slick. All the chakra colors were represented. Too bad it was wreaking havoc because it was kind of pretty to look at.

Corinne appeared by my side. "What is that?"

"A chakra demon," I said. "It's responsible for your mother's condition."

Corinne's jaw tightened. "Tell me how I can help."

"I need to keep the area clear while Neville and I work to capture it," I said. "I don't want anyone to get hurt."

Corinne let loose a shrill whistle. "Supers, we need to move! The fury needs her space!"

"Do we have to use labels?" I asked. "You could just say my name."

Corinne scrunched her nose. "Your name is Fury."

Oh, right.

While Corinne successfully herded the mourners off to the side, I ran through my game plan. I considered using my siphoning power to concentrate all the present witches' power in me, but with chakras off balance, it seemed too risky. I could end up an emotional basket case incapable of defeating my own demons, let alone the one standing in front of me.

"What are you waiting for, Eden?" my mother asked. "An invitation?"

The hazy rainbow began to swirl.

"Oh no you don't! Party's over, Chakra Khan," I said.

"Chakra *demon*," Neville corrected me.

I cut him a glance. "Eighties reference, Neville. Keep up."

The colors sharpened and glowed and I knew the demon was trying to work its mojo on me. Emotions began slipping and sliding. The memory of Tanner and Sassy flooded my senses. Their betrayal. And my mother's.

"Nope," I said. "Not going to happen." I could feel the pull along my spine, as though the demon was physically trying to rearrange bits of it. "My energy pools are staying exactly as they are, thanks."

The demon didn't speak. I felt my spine relax and knew it had released whatever foothold it was trying to gain, yet the bands of color continued to spin and glow as though the demon was still hard at work.

I quickly realized the reason why.

I turned to see old ladies in black dresses creep closer to me from where Corinne had sequestered them. The demon planned to use the mourners to attack me by influencing their chakras. It hadn't occurred to me that it could bring out the violent side of residents, but of course that made sense.

"Eden Fury, you step away from that chakra demon or you're going to be in a world of pain," Adele warned. Her eyes burned with anger.

I hesitated. No way could I fight a coven of witches without someone getting hurt, which was exactly what I'd hoped to avoid.

"Look over here, Eden," Grandma called. "I'm being irreverent!" She climbed onto the casket and began to belt Led Zeppelin's *Immigrant Song* at the top of her lungs.

I looked at the demon. "Uh, I think you might've moved the wrong chakra there." Thank the gods because the thought of fighting Grandma was enough to put me in a coma.

My mother ran to the casket and I thought she was going to force Grandma to come down. Instead I heard her say, "I know I don't say it often enough, but you're the best mother in all the realms." She held up her arms for a hug.

Grandma looked down at her. "Go fill up your love tank somewhere else. Can't you see I'm busy singing up here?"

"Love me," my mother screeched, wriggling her fingers.

Aunt Thora sat in a chair and wept. "Why doesn't my daughter ever visit?" she wailed.

She rarely mentioned Uncle Moyer's sister. I didn't even realize it bothered her that her daughter left Chipping Cheddar and never looked back. Like I would have if I hadn't sunk my temporary fangs into Fergus.

I turned back to the demon. "I guess you can't control an army if you can't control which way their chakras will shift. Tough luck."

"It won't take an army to defeat you, darling," Adele said. "One strong witch will do the trick."

The demon's colors began to stretch and swirl around the circle. It was gearing up for another kind of attack.

"I can't decide what to do," Corinne said. Her gaze darted around. "Do I help attack the demon? Do I help my grandmother? Do I make sure Esther doesn't fall off the casket and break a hip?"

Great. Analysis paralysis. Not what I needed during a fight.

"Neville," I called. "A little help!"

"Doing what, O wondrous one?" he called back in a singsong voice.

Sometimes the wizard was the smartest guy in the room but not today. "I need the crystals!"

"Oh, right." He patted his pockets until he located the bottomless bag. "They're all in here. Deceptive, isn't it?"

"Can you be proud of your invention later? I'm in the middle of a situation."

He tossed the bag across the circle and I caught it with one hand. I emptied the bag of crystals into my open palm and said the incantation that Neville had gotten from our friends in Mexico. It was in Spanish so I had no idea what I was saying, but I plowed ahead. I threw the crystals into the air and hoped for the best. I watched in awe as each band of color got sucked into the corresponding crystal—red, orange, yellow, green, blue, indigo and violet.

"The demon version of drawing and quartering," Neville said cheerfully. He gathered up the demon-infused crystals and placed them back in the bottomless bag. "This will serve until the extraction team arrives."

I finally released the breath I'd been holding. "Thanks, Neville. You've been a huge help."

"De nada," he said. "I'll alert the Mexican office that the demon has been captured."

"What happens to the crystals once they're back in Otherworld?" I asked.

"According to protocol, the pieces of the demon will be released so that it can reform. It's considered cruel and unusual punishment to keep it apart."

"What about the crystals?" I asked.

"They'll be returned to headquarters in time." He shrugged. "Could take months. You know how bureaucracy is."

Now that the chakra demon was safely separated and encapsulated, I was able to focus on the scene around me. Some mourners were sobbing. Some were recovering from angry meltdowns. Grandma sat on the casket, her legs dangling over the side, while she happily played what could only be Little Critters on her phone.

"Grandma, you should probably get down now," I said. I walked over and offered a hand to help her. "Poor Myrtle."

Grandma took my hand and jumped to the ground. "Are you kidding? Myrtle doesn't know how lucky she is. This funeral was way more exciting than anything that happened to her in life."

"Drunk Myrtle would have loved it," Aunt Thora said.

My mother blinked as she looked around the hillside in a daze. "I feel emotionally exhausted."

"No kidding," Grandma said. "You should've seen yourself. It was just like when you were a baby begging for my attention."

"Which you never gave," my mother said bitterly.

"You were a baby," Grandma said. "It doesn't get much more boring than that."

"Grandma!" I admonished her.

"Wait until you have kids of your own," Grandma said knowingly. "You'll see."

If I was going to be anything like Grandma as a mother, I had no business reproducing.

Adele and Corinne approached us, maintaining a reasonable distance from my family. "Well done, Eden," Adele said. "How wonderful to see you in action. I have to admit, I wasn't certain what to expect when you arrived to replace Paul Pidcock, but I'm convinced that we couldn't have done better."

"Well, you couldn't have done worse," Grandma said.

"Thanks for the vote of confidence," I said.

My mother played with her statement necklace. "What do you think? Should someone say a few final words or has that ship sailed?"

"I think Myrtle would be satisfied with a closing song," Grandma said. She tapped her phone screen.

"No Led Zeppelin, Grandma," I said. "This is Myrtle's funeral, not yours."

"Relax," Grandma said. "I've got it covered." She tapped the screen again and Frank Sinatra began to croon.

"Oh, I love this song," my mother said, and started to sing along. "Fly me to the moon..."

The next thing I knew the mourners had joined hands

around the casket and were singing about flying to the moon and playing among the stars. Most of them were horribly off key, but it didn't matter.

Grandma's gaze flicked to the casket for a final look. "Myrtle would approve," she said.

CHAPTER NINETEEN

IT HAD BEEN a couple of days since the chakra demon was returned safely to Otherworld and I was updating the list of those affected to make sure that everyone was back to normal before I sent my report to headquarters. Ted O'Neill had described Father Kevin's return as nothing short of a miracle.

"Is there any way to get my mom's chakras back *into* alignment?" Meg had asked, when I'd called the house to check on Julie. "I liked the new version better."

"Are you sure about that? You seemed uncomfortable with her Zen attitude."

"I guess it is nice to have someone worry about me."

Corinne had texted to say that Rosalie had regained her sight and was behaving normally—well, normally for Rosalie.

I was in the barn inspecting John's progress after a full day of work when a hesitant Clara poked her head in the entrance.

"Would it be okay if I came in?" she asked. "I understand if you'd rather not speak to me."

"Get in here, goofball. Am I happy to see you!" I said.

Relief rippled across her pretty features. "You are?"

I crossed the barn to hug her. "Of course I am. I was so worried you'd have a heart attack."

"But I was so awful to you," she said. She squeezed once and released me. "Oh. There are a lot of positive emotions there." She sounded surprised.

"It wasn't you. It was the chakra demon," I said. "I know you didn't mean it. You weren't yourself."

She fidgeted with the hem of her shirt. "I might have meant some of it."

I balked. "You did?"

"The chakra imbalance made me heartless, not a liar," she said. "Obviously I didn't mean the horrible stuff, but the things I said about you and your family…I do think you're too hard on them sometimes."

"Clara, you don't know everything I know."

"I realize that, but the reality seems to be that they've mellowed," Clara said. "It doesn't absolve them of past crimes, of course, but they don't seem to be scorching the earth the way they used to."

No, that much was true. "There's something I need to tell you about Tanner."

"Sassy forgave me for what I said about him, thankfully."

"It's not about that. It's about what happened in high school."

Clara frowned. "I thought you were over that."

"It's not that simple." I sank onto a wooden stool that John left behind. "Tanner didn't act of his own free will."

Clara rolled her eyes. "Eden, you're not going to paint Sassy as the femme fatale he couldn't resist, are you? That's not your style."

I covered my face with my hands. "That's not what I mean." I slid my hands back to my sides and looked at her. "It was a hex. My mother hexed him so that he would sleep with Sassy."

Clara blinked rapidly, as though her eyelashes were responsible for processing information. "Why would she do that to you?"

"Because she didn't want me involved with a human," I said. "Apparently she was willing to play dirty to make that happen." Not that I should be surprised. She was evil, after all.

Clara put a hand on the wall to steady herself. "I can't believe it. How did you find out?"

"Aunt Thora's imbalanced chakra told me."

"Oh, Eden. I'm so sorry. That changes everything."

"Well, not everything," I said. "Tanner is still a jerk and Sassy is too good for him."

"I know, but what if that had never happened," Clara said. "Would he and Sassy be together now? It changed the course of history."

I nodded. "And I can't even tell Sassy because she doesn't know about the supernatural world."

"I'm not sure I'd tell Sassy anyway," Clara said. "What's done is done. What did your mom say when you confronted her?"

"I haven't." Yet.

Clara whistled. "This could escalate to a very unpleasant degree."

"I'll send up a flare to warn you." I inhaled deeply. "What about Chief Fox? Do you still think I'm wrong to hide our relationship?"

She lowered her gaze. "No, I don't. Your family doesn't approve and there would be consequences. Clearly."

"I'd like to think they'd stay out of my business at my age, but I know better."

"Yeah, and I think you and the chief have something real. I'd hate to see them tamper with it."

I gave her a rueful smile. "Same."

"Too bad you couldn't accidentally zap her during Myrtle's funeral," Clara said. "You could have gotten your revenge without her realizing it."

"My revenge is to outshine her at her own funeral," I said. "She'd hate that." We both laughed. "While we're on the subject, what do you think you would say at my funeral?"

"Yours? Making plans for the future?"

I shrugged. "I've already died a few times. One of these times could be the last. Might as well be ready."

"Have you forgotten about the whole immortality thing?" Clara asked.

"Hey, a vampire can be staked," I said. "I'm sure there's a way to rid the world of a fury if someone was ambitious enough."

"Let's not dwell on unpleasant thoughts," she said. "Now that my chakras are back in alignment, I'm liable to overcompensate on the compassion." She threw her arms around me and kissed my cheek. "Ugh, I hate how I treated you. Can we just put a barrier around the town to keep all these demons out?"

"Unfortunately, nobody has that kind of power." And I'd be out of a job, which wasn't necessarily a bad thing.

"Is this a secret meeting or can anyone join?" Chief Fox's perfect form graced the doorway of the barn and my spirits lifted.

"You're not just anyone," I said. "You're my boyfriend."

"Your secret boyfriend," he said with a wink.

I felt a pang of guilt, but I quickly shoved it aside.

"I should be going," Clara said. "I have an appointment at the…place where I need to be."

"Good luck with that," I said.

"Nice to see you again, Clara," the chief said, as she passed him. He sauntered into the barn, whistling as he walked.

"What put you in such a good mood?" I asked.

He planted a kiss on my lips. "You. What else?"

"I battled a chakra demon at Myrtle's funeral because it was wreaking havoc on half the town," I said.

"I knew something had happened. The mayor gave up her parking spot and issued a formal apology. She seemed mortified."

I nodded. "It won't get easier to be chief, now that you know. In some ways, I've made your life more difficult."

"Worth it," he said.

I gave an involuntary shudder. He had no idea that was what my mother and Grandma liked to say on the occasions when they eviscerated each other.

"You sure you don't want to go back to Iowa where it's safer?"

"I didn't become the chief of police because I like to play it safe," he said.

"Why did you?" I asked.

"What? Become a cop?" He stuffed his hands in his pockets. "I wanted to help people and I look pretty good in a uniform."

"No dark past where you're secretly seeking revenge for the death of your first wife?"

"Why would I be looking in Chipping Cheddar?" He broke into a broad grin. "I'm kidding! There's no wife, murdered or otherwise."

I brushed my fingers against his rugged jaw. "Are you sure there aren't any deep, dark secrets?"

He chuckled. "I'm a Boy Scout. I'm sorry. I could tell you about the time I rode a friend's motorcycle and got a ticket for not wearing a helmet."

"Is that true?"

He lowered his head. "No, sorry. Iowa doesn't require that riders wear a helmet."

I sighed. "Even your lies are lame."

"Excuse me, miss. Are you calling the chief of police lame?"

"I liked you better when I thought you were a stripper."

He started to unbutton his shirt. "Don't give me any ideas."

I placed a hand over his to stop him. "You strip naked in this barn and one of us is going to end up in the hospital. I promise you it won't be me."

He laughed. "You really are worried about someone finding out about us."

I remained silent. I couldn't explain how important it was without telling him more than he needed to know.

"I should go back to the house before someone comes looking for me." The last thing I needed was my mother or Grandma darkening this doorway and seeing me kiss the chief. John was going to have to start working overtime to get this place finished.

The chief inclined his head. "I'd like you to do something for me before I go."

"What's that?"

"I want to see it all, the full display, and I'd like you to stay that way until I've finished."

A lump formed in my throat. "Finished?"

"Admiring you," he said. He ran a hand down my shoulder blade. "Let me see the real you, Eden."

"This is the real me. Besides, you've seen my wings."

"I want the whole kit and caboodle. The Medusa wig. The good, the bad, and the ugly."

I folded my arms. "Why?"

"Because I don't want you to feel ashamed or embarrassed of who you are. I want to show you that I accept all of you, not just the parts you deem worthy."

I hesitated. "What if you don't?"

"Don't what?"

"Accept all of me," I said. "What if you take a long look at me in all my gory glory and decide you're not interested?"

He cupped my chin in his hand. "Do you really think that's possible?"

"I wouldn't blame you."

His expression softened and he gently ran his fingers through a ribbon of my hair. "Show me."

Against my better judgment, I uncloaked. The black wings sprouted, the snakes uncoiled, and the eyes flamed. He took a startled step backward when one of the snakes stuck its head between us and hissed right in his face.

"Hello to you, too," he said, greeting the snake. He reclaimed his position directly in front of me. "Look on the bright side, you're never alone."

"How is that a bright side? I like my own company." I preferred it to most other people or supernaturals, in fact.

Chief Fox addressed the snake. "Would you mind giving us a little space? I'm going to kiss her now and I'd rather not get a fang stuck in my cheek for the effort."

I suppressed a laugh as the snake returned to rest on top of my head. "You want to kiss me like this?"

"I want to do more than kiss you, but slow and steady wins the race."

I inched closer. "We're turtles now?"

"I don't know. Is that in your wheelhouse?"

I laughed before I could stop myself. "Turtle shifting? Not really."

He tried to wrap his arms around me, but they got stuck in the feathers of the wings. "Is there a YouTube tutorial on this?"

"Probably."

He stroked the wings. "They're softer than they look, like you. And the color...That's the deepest black I've ever seen."

"Like my soul?"

"I don't know. I haven't glimpsed it yet, but I'll keep trying." He locked eyes with me. "You're so beautiful, Eden."

"I will be as soon as you let me cloak these monstrosities." And maybe brush my hair. Ugh, I was starting to sound like my mother even in my head.

"No," he said softly. "Just like this." His lips brushed against mine and I felt the snakes on my head stiffen, as though waiting to see if he was friend or foe—or something else entirely.

As his fingers threaded through the feathers, I sank into the kiss and became acutely aware of the rapid beating of my heart. Soon enough, everything faded away. I forgot all about wings and snakes and immortality. There was only the blur of our two bodies combined and I no longer knew where one ended and the other began.

And that was fine with me.

* * *

Keep an eye out for book 7 in the Federal Bureau of Magic series!

ALSO BY ANNABEL CHASE

Thank you for reading ***Three Alarm Fury***! Sign up for my newsletter and receive a FREE Starry Hollow Witches short story— http://eepurl.com/ctYNzf. You can also like me on Facebook so you can find out about the next book before it's even available.

Other books by Annabel Chase include:

Starry Hollow Witches

Magic & Murder, Book 1

Magic & Mystery, Book 2

Magic & Mischief, Book 3

Magic & Mayhem, Book 4

Magic & Mercy, Book 5

Magic & Madness, Book 6

Magic & Malice, Book 7

Magic & Mythos, Book 8

Magic & Mishaps, Book 9

Magic & Maladies, Book 10

Spellbound Paranormal Cozy Mysteries

Curse the Day, Book 1

Doom and Broom, Book 2

Spell's Bells, Book 3

Lucky Charm, Book 4

Better Than Hex, Book 5

Cast Away, Book 6

A Touch of Magic, Book 7

A Drop in the Potion, Book 8

Hemlocked and Loaded, Book 9

All Spell Breaks Loose, Book 10

Spellbound Ever After

Crazy For Brew, Book 1

Lost That Coven Feeling, Book 2

Wands Upon A Time, Book 3

Charmed Offensive, Book 4

Poetry in Potion, Book 5

Made in the USA
Las Vegas, NV
09 May 2021